Real Good

Anna E. Sapp
104 Dixie Ave.
Campbellsville, KY 42718

Rob wondered if his emotions had been that obvious.

The empathy in Vanessa's concerned blue eyes almost unnerved him. His arms ached to hold her, and he suspected that, were they alone, nothing would keep him from putting his arms around her. But he couldn't do that, not here in the presence of the girls.

And not without having at least some idea of how Vanessa really felt about him—and how she'd respond!

He blinked hard to clear his vision and, hopefully, to clear his mind. Her head tilted in that questioning way he'd begun to recognize.

"Headache, Rob?"

He grinned slightly. *What would she say or do if I were to admit it was my heart, rather than my head, giving me difficulties?*

D1374271

Books by Eileen Berger

Love Inspired

A Family for Andi #57
A Special Kind of Family #132

EILEEN BERGER

has been writing for many years, mostly children's stories and poetry when her daughter and two sons were small, before having hundreds of other manuscripts published. She had been happy growing up on a farm, then living for a time in two major American cities, but feels blessed to continue living in the same north-central Pennsylvania town, Hughesville, where she and her husband, Bob, raised their now-grown children.

She is active in writing circles as speaker, teacher, board member, panelist, conference director and contest coordinator, but is especially grateful for the West Branch Christian Writers, the wonderful critique/support group without which she says she might never have gotten even the first of her six novels published.

A Special Kind of Family
Eileen Berger

Love Inspired®

Published by Steeple Hill Books™

If you purchased this book without a cover you should be aware
that this book is stolen property. It was reported as "unsold and
destroyed" to the publisher, and neither the author nor the
publisher has received any payment for this "stripped book."

 STEEPLE HILL BOOKS

Steeple
Hill™

ISBN 0-373-87139-2

A SPECIAL KIND OF FAMILY

Copyright © 2001 by Eileen M. Berger

All rights reserved. Except for use in any review, the reproduction
or utilization of this work in whole or in part in any form by any
electronic, mechanical or other means, now known or hereafter
invented, including xerography, photocopying and recording, or in
any information storage or retrieval system, is forbidden without
the written permission of the editorial office, Steeple Hill Books,
300 East 42nd Street, New York, NY 10017 U.S.A.

All characters in this book have no existence outside the imagination of
the author and have no relation whatsoever to anyone bearing the same
name or names. They are not even distantly inspired by any individual
known or unknown to the author, and all incidents are pure invention.

This edition published by arrangement with Steeple Hill Books.

® and TM are trademarks of Steeple Hill Books, used under license.
Trademarks indicated with ® are registered in the United States Patent
and Trademark Office, the Canadian Trade Marks Office and in other
countries.

Visit us at www.steeplehill.com

Printed in U.S.A.

There is a time for everything, and a season
for every activity under heaven...a time to heal...
—*Ecclesiastes* 3: 1, 3

To—
Vicki, Jim and Bill,

Our children who, while growing up,
never seemed to notice that a typewriter on the
dining-room table was not a usual part of their
friends' decor. You have given your father and me
much joy and reasons for thankfulness.

We dearly love you.

Chapter One

Although it wasn't quite dark yet, streetlights were already glimmering by the time Vanessa McHenry drove into town. Because she had worked late, there had been only a few minutes to visit at the hospital with her cousin, Keith, his wife, and their new baby; Gram wouldn't be able to leave to see her newborn great-granddaughter until Vanessa came to relieve her.

She always enjoyed the small-town ambiance of wide sidewalks overhung by yellow-and red-leafed maples, some branching in an archway above macadamized Main Street. But as she passed the cross-street she abruptly stopped humming along with her car radio; the red Sylvan Falls Volunteer Fire Company ambulance looked frighteningly out of place in front of Gram's big, white, early-Victorian house.

She parked hastily, and was just getting out of her car when AnnaMae came running down the porch steps. "Oh, Vanessa! Gram fell—they think her hip's broken!"

Oh, no—not Gram! "What happened?" She, too, was running now, horrified at this happening to the woman they all loved.

"She was up on a chair, reaching for a dish on the top shelf of one of the kitchen cabinets." AnnaMae's hand slid into Vanessa's as they hurried up the steps. "I called 911, like she told me to."

"That's good—just what I'd have done had I been here." Gram's girls, as she usually thought of them, needed a lot of building up.

"We tried to get hold of you at your office and at your apartment—Gram wanted you to come right away, and to bring stuff so you could stay overnight with us—or at least till we find out how bad she is."

They were inside, through the hallway, and Rob Corland looked up from where he and another man knelt beside Gram on the kitchen's off-white linoleum. "We're almost sure the hip's fractured, Van."

Her brief smile as she dropped to her knees beside him was meant to convey gratitude for his help and for the information, but she turned away quickly, leaning over her grandmother. "Are you having an awful lot of pain?"

"Not *too* bad—when I don't move." She appeared fairly calm, but there were fine vertical lines between her salt-and-pepper brows and at the outer corners of her eyes.

Rob gave the older woman's hand a reassuring squeeze. "We'll be as gentle as possible, Gram, but we must get you onto this firm stretcher and to the emergency room. Maybe X rays will show you're just bruised."

It wasn't strange that he'd call her Gram; many people who weren't related did so. Looking around, Vanessa saw the worry on the faces of the five girls who were hovering as near as possible. Getting to her feet, she drew them away so the men could do whatever was necessary.

Jana Jenson, the wide-eyed seventeen-year-old, blurted, "I said *I'd* get that dish for her, but..."

Gram's firm voice interjected with, "There's no way I'd let you—*any* of you—climb up on a chair in your condition!"

Vanessa forced herself to refrain from mentioning the folding step stool she'd bought last year, or that Jana, though about six months pregnant, probably wouldn't have fallen. "I'll follow the ambulance to the hospital...."

"Oh, no, dear." Gram wasn't missing a thing. "You're needed here."

She sucked in her breath and nodded slowly, knowing that, according to the rules, some responsible adult must, indeed, be present in a supervisory capacity. All six of them followed the men out onto the large porch, down the steps and to the curb, where they watched Gram being lifted into the ambulance.

Rob turned. "I've been praying for her ever since we got the call, Van, and will keep on doing that—for all of you." His dark-brown eyes were warm with sincerity and concern as they looked down into hers. "I'll call if I learn anything, but I won't be able to stay at the hospital very long."

"Thanks, Rob. I do appreciate you and Pete coming right away, and taking such good care of her," she replied, including the younger man in her smile. Rob's authority and calm manner had helped her as much as it did Gram and the others. She added with a twinge of nostalgia, "I remember, when we were dating, your taking all those EMT classes so you could volunteer while not working at the funeral home."

He was inside the vehicle, making adjustments, busy with things she couldn't even guess at. He grinned at Gram, although he seemed to be obliquely responding to Vanessa's words, "Otherwise, I wouldn't get to sit here beside you and hold your hand as we go for a ride."

Vanessa couldn't make out Gram's reply, but it didn't sound upset. Moisture came into her eyes as he pulled the rear doors closed and the ambulance started to move. She looked around at the girls with her, seeing tears running down their cheeks as they continued calling goodbyes.

She cleared her throat, not wanting them to suspect she was every bit as concerned as they. "I suppose you've eaten, but I haven't. Let's go see what's in the freezer. Gram usually has ice cream, so perhaps we can make sundaes."

"Or milkshakes," Kate Frye countered.

"That sounds good, too." Vanessa was fairly sure the girl was simply trying for some feeling of normalcy. "And there's probably popcorn, at least Gram used to always keep it on hand."

They trooped up the steps, through the huge front doorway with its imposing fan-shaped glass at the top and a tall panel at each side, and entered the large hallway leading to the kitchen at the far left corner of the house.

Vanessa already knew the girls, for she'd been involved ever since Gram first spoke of opening her home to young women unable or unwilling to keep their babies, yet not choosing to abort them.

Keith's wife, Andi, and her father had provided the grant money, but Vanessa did most of the leg-work necessary to bring it into being—and she was still amazed that her brilliant lawyer-mother, who usually seemed so cool and uncaring, had volunteered to handle all legal matters!

Kate had been the first to move in, recommended by the pastor of a church in a nearby city. Almost twenty, she was the oldest; the next, a year younger, was AnnaMae, whose parents wanted nothing more to do with her because of her "grievous sin." Ricki, also 19, had been told she had to leave home if she didn't agree to an abortion. Vanessa felt especially bad for Jana and Barbara, both 17 and still in high school.

As they took care of getting the food, Vanessa called Andi's room in the obstetrics department. "I'm relieved you're still at the hospital, Keith," she began as her favorite cousin picked up the phone. "I'm at Gram's. She fell in the kitchen, and we think her hip's broken."

"I'll be right there!"

She recognized the apprehension in his voice, and shook her head, although he couldn't see that, of course. "I have to stay with the girls, but the ambulance is on its way there, to the Emergency Room.''

''Who's on this evening?''

''Rob Corland's in charge. He handled things really well, I think. And Gram didn't appear worried once she knew I'd stay overnight.''

''I'm sorry that's necessary, Van.''

''It's the least I can do.''

There was a slow exhalation before his next words. ''I'll go down to the ER right away, and stay with her through X rays and whatever they have to do.''

''Keith? You'll let us know as soon as you find out anything?''

''Of course.''

The girls had waited for Vanessa to finish the call and join them. AnnaMae stopped Jana as she picked up her spoon to begin her vanilla ice cream island in its sea of chocolate syrup. ''Shouldn't we pray for Gram before we eat?''

There were nods and the sound of shuffling feet beneath the table as she added, ''And remember, Gram says we've got to believe that God *can* heal, and that He wants us to keep praying, to keep talking to Him about everything.''

She turned toward Vanessa. ''How about you praying out loud?''

Vanessa did precious little praying anymore—

although she'd been desperately doing some within these past minutes. She figured she probably had little right to ask for anything, anyway, as her prayers had often been prompted by situations she might have avoided. "Why don't you, AnnaMae, since it's your idea?"

AnnaMae's long, dark-brown hair slid forward over her shoulders as she bent her head. "Dear God, please take care of Gram. She's such a *good* person and we love her a lot. I guess we should have tried harder to keep her from getting up on that chair, but she didn't want any of us to get hurt."

Vanessa heard what sounded like a choked sob on her right, and reached to squeeze Barb's hand as AnnaMae continued, "We'd sure like You to make her hip not broken, God, but if it is, help it to not hurt *too* bad, and help it get fixed and heal real fast. Amen." She did not look around, but picked up her spoon and moved it about in her dish before raising ice cream to her lips.

That was a prayer Vanessa could relate to, short and saying exactly what it was meant to.

She should have phoned Dad before eating, and Uncle Isaac, and Aunt Phyllis, so she finished quickly and made those calls. She found that Dad was away, not expected back until tomorrow, but Mother would try to contact him tonight. Uncle

Isaac said he'd leave for the hospital immediately, and her aunt, already at the hospital as second shift nursing supervisor, would go check on Gram. In addition, Aunt Phyl would come to Gram's the next morning, when Vanessa would need to leave for work.

Vanessa understood the girls' wanting to stay up until they learned how Gram was making out, so she agreed. They watched two half-hour TV comedies before receiving Keith's call.

"I'm sorry to have kept you waiting so long, but her hip *is* broken, as we thought. She's in Room 417, and has had pain medication. Her heart, blood pressure and everything else are good, thank God, and Dr. Rosemont, the orthopedic surgeon, hopes to operate in a day or two."

"I hope he can!" Vanessa passed on this information to the anxious girls, then asked if he'd be staying much longer.

"No, Gram's getting drowsy, probably from the medicine, but I'll stop again in the morning on my way to work, after I check in with Andi and our adorable little Katherine."

She could almost hear the smile in his voice. This was the way it was supposed to be when you loved someone, wasn't it? "Sleep well, Keith. And kiss your daughter for me when you see her."

"Sure will, Van. With pleasure!"

* * *

Vanessa rolled over to push in the alarm button ten minutes before it was set to ring, and was ready for the day by the time Jana and Barb got downstairs, dressed for school. They'd said the night before that all they wanted for breakfast was fruit, hot chocolate and cornflakes, so she had that waiting for them on the kitchen table.

The other three were at the table by the time Aunt Phyllis Bastian arrived. "I stopped to see Mom and talked with one of her nurses just before I left this morning. She had a fairly good night, considering everything."

That didn't satisfy Jana. "Does she still hurt so awful much?"

"Quite a bit, I'm afraid." Her smile was somewhat rueful. "But she made me promise before I left that I'd tell everyone she's doing just fine!"

Barb's hazel eyes were round with worry. "You mean—she's *not?*"

"She's doing well for someone her age." Phyl's arm slid around the girl's shoulders. "And you know Gram, she's convinced everything will work out okay."

Barb looked even more upset. "She *is* going to be all right, isn't she?"

"*Sure,* she is." Vanessa picked up her small purse and keys. "I must get to work. How about my dropping you and Jana off at school on my way?''

They grabbed their books and ran out ahead of her, as she'd hoped they would, and she was in her office within a few minutes of dropping them at school. Time flew with in-house matters to be taken care of immediately, then fax, e-mail, and phone messages to be answered.

She hardly glanced at a clock until Keith called around one-thirty to tell her Gram's surgery was scheduled for the following morning. Vanessa wanted to let Rob know—actually, she wanted to hear his reassuring voice—but the funeral home's answering machine gave the very proper message recorded by his partner stating that the service for some man was taking place at two that afternoon. Her call would be returned if she left a name and number.

She did that, then leaned back in her chair and punched in the number for Gram's room. The connection went through quickly. ''Good afternoon, how are you feeling?''

A soft laugh. ''Grateful, mostly.''

''Grateful?'' That wasn't the word she'd have used.

''Mm-hmmm. My fall could have happened anytime, you know, but it took place when the girls were right there, and AnnaMae made the calls, and

Rob and Pete came right away, and you stayed overnight—why *shouldn't* I be grateful?''

Vanessa felt a crooked smile come to her own face. "Why not indeed?" But she wondered how many others would have reacted that way. "I understand that you're scheduled for hip surgery tomorrow morning."

"Right. And look, dear, don't think you must be with me. Your primary responsibility has got to be there in Sylvan Falls."

She knew Gram wasn't referring to her job here at the plant. "Things went well last night. I stayed until Aunt Phyl came this morning, and dropped Jana and Barb off at school on my way here. Everyone's fine."

"I've been wondering about this afternoon, though. Phyl will need to leave no later than two-thirty to get back here for her shift at the hospital."

Vanessa drew in a deep breath. "I was hoping to get away early, but there's no way I can leave until at *least* four-thirty or five."

"I'm going to call Gin Redding. Perhaps she can cover for us since she lives just across the side yard."

Us, not *you*. Dear Gram, worrying about everything at home when she's got enough problems there. "That would help, of course, but I hate to make you do the phoning."

"Now you just get back to what you have to do, dear. I'll call Gin, and if she can't come over I'll ask another friend. I'm sure to find someone."

There was the click of a closed line, and Vanessa sat there for a moment looking at the phone still in her hand. Leaning forward, she replaced it and got to her feet. She made a practice of getting around to each department every day, convinced that being readily accessible avoided the necessity of spending a lot more time troubleshooting.

She was almost disappointed that Rob had not returned her call by the time she left at 5:28. With her mind on getting to Gram's as soon as possible, and staying there, she'd verified that one of the foremen would receive any after-hours emergency calls. She considered stopping to pick up pizza on the way but had not had time to call ahead; she'd better hurry to relieve Gram's good-hearted neighbor.

As she parked by the curb and hurried inside, Vanessa was still trying to decide what to have for dinner—and gave a sigh of relief when Gin told her that church members would be sending the evening meal each day until further notice. She knew Gram often did this for others, but had not considered a possible reversal of that kindness.

The doorbell rang, and Ricki hurried to respond.

"Hi, Mr. Corland. So you're the first to bring us a meal!"

"I guess I am." He chuckled. "Want to take a couple of these?"

Going into the hallway, Vanessa was surprised to see his arms filled with a number of take-out boxes from her favorite steak house. "I hope everyone's hungry," he was saying even before she could greet him. "I brought both steak and barbecued chicken from Jerry's Barbeque."

Does he remember the two of us going there? It seems so long ago!

Barb and Jana also insisted on carrying containers to the kitchen, so he was empty-handed as she said, "Just set everything on the table till we get organized."

They exclaimed over the abundance of not only the meat, vegetables and salads, but even cherry and apple pies. Vanessa asked, "Have you eaten, Rob?"

"Well, the church served a luncheon following the interment, and the family asked us to join them...."

"You and Gin will stay and eat with us," Vanessa stated briskly. "There's so much food."

With the girls working together, it was only minutes until the table was set, coffee and hot water ready, the food on serving platters and everyone seated. At first the conversation primarily concerned Gram's scheduled surgery, and the length of time anticipated for recovery and rehabilitation before she could return home.

Kate's grandmother had died the year before, so she asked all kinds of questions about Rob's work as a mortician. Vanessa tried several times to turn the conversation to something more pleasant, but the girl kept coming back to that subject.

Jana and Barb talked about Sylvan Falls, comparing the school and community here with their own—but said little about families and friends they'd left to come here.

Rob's pager beeped as they were eating dessert, and Vanessa was sorry to hear him say, "Yes, I'll be there as quickly as possible."

Vanessa walked out to the porch with Rob and thanked him again for bringing dinner. "My pleasure, Van." His hand reached for hers and gave it a firm squeeze. "It's been a long time since we ate a meal together."

She nodded—and felt almost bereft when he released her hand.

"I must hurry home and change into something less casual than jeans and sweatshirt. I'm expected to look professional when I go to the hospital for someone. You remember Nate Bowman, don't you?"

"Of course. He was an especially good friend of Grandad's, one of his buddies." Being reminded of her grandfather still gave her that clutching pain in her stomach. *Another fireman dead! He was one of those who tried to rescue Grandad, and now he's gone, too. I hope Gram doesn't know, for that would make her feel even worse.*

The girls were already putting away leftovers and loading the dishwasher when Vanessa walked back into the house after bidding Rob goodnight. In spite of the conversation and activities with the girls, she felt more alone with him gone.

But she wouldn't dwell on her own feelings; Gram had asked her to check the homework of the younger girls and make sure the older ones studied for their General Equivalency Diploma exams.

None of the three who were old enough to graduate from high school had done so. Ricki would have last June, near the head of her class, had she not run off with her "one true love," who was in the army and stationed in the Midwest. He had not married her, as he'd said he was going to—and now denied paternity.

Kate dropped out of school after her junior year, going to work at a fast-food place, "...to make money, have a car, and stuff like that." AnnaMae admitted to having been in a state of rebellion; education was so overwhelmingly important to her parents that no matter what grades she got or what she achieved, nothing was "good enough." She'd eventually stopped studying or doing assignments and deliberately got poor marks.

Vanessa related especially to that; she had not stopped studying—and even graduated second in her class, but she'd rebelled in other ways. Looking back, she was ashamed of deliberately hanging around people her age and older who were known for drinking, wild driving and other questionable activities, including marijuana use.

It was a phase that had not lasted long, thank goodness; she had not fit in there, but remained on the sidelines, something of a nonjudging bystander, not actively participating in much of what was going on, but being associated with them in people's minds. *But I did get Mother's attention, and succeeded in upsetting her as much as she upset me....*

Gram had stressed how essential it was for the girls to study hard and get their GEDs, so Vanessa struggled to remember algebraic fundamentals forgotten since high school—and began to realize what her grandmother was involved with every day!

While checking homework for the younger two, she reminded them all that Gram's rules, which they'd agreed to when coming here, were still in effect, including being in bed early on week nights. They hurried into pajamas and came back downstairs in time to watch TV for thirty minutes.

As it turned out, she did permit them some leeway, since they were upset to learn that Gram's fracture was so severe, and she would be undergoing surgery the next day.

The older three usually had an extra hour before they were required to be in their rooms. She'd expected to go upstairs soon after them, and when the phone rang, she dreaded to pick it up. Hearing Rob's voice she sank back into the recliner with relief—or something more?

"I hope this isn't too late to be calling, Van?"

She laughed. "Not too late since it's *you*." But then, realizing how that might sound, she sat up straighter, explaining, "I was afraid it was the hospital—that something might be wrong there. Or perhaps it would be a problem at work."

"Nope. Just me." His voice was reassuring. "I wondered if you might have any more news, so I called to check before turning in for the night."

They spoke of various other things, too, especially Nate Bowman's wife and two daughters, who were holding up quite well, perhaps partly because he'd been in the nursing home so long before his death.

She was pleased when Rob admitted, "Actually,

my main reason for calling was to thank you again for inviting me to stay for dinner. I enjoyed being with you."

Is he just being polite? "We appreciated your company as much as the food you brought." She had deliberately used *we* instead of *I.*

"It brought back a lot of memories...."

Yes, it did!

Chapter Two

Vanessa expected the morning's routine to be similar to the day before, but shortly after she got downstairs, Mrs. Redding came across the yard, offering to stay until Aunt Phyl arrived. "...In case you want to go around to visit your grandmother on the way to work," she told Vanessa.

She blinked back unexpected tears at Gin's generosity. "I'd been wishing I could see her before her surgery. And may I ask another favor? I know Gram's accident was already on the prayer chain, but could you start it again, saying that surgery is scheduled for ten o'clock and asking for prayers?"

"Rob put it on already." Her hand was pressing firmly against Vanessa's waist. "So *you* get going."

It was a perfect autumn day, every direction she looked revealing countless shades of red, yellow, orange, even wine, elegantly set off by evergreens. This was her favorite season, and she recalled Gram saying last Sunday at a family get-together, "Each year I think God can't make it any more beautiful, but He outdid Himself this October!"

The hills and mountains made Vanessa glad to be living here in north-central Pennsylvania. Gram kept thanking God for all this, but if He was really as all-powerful and all-knowing as she thought, wouldn't He already know how much people enjoyed it?

Once she arrived at the hospital, it didn't take Vanessa long to find Gram's room. She sat on the edge of Gram's hospital bed, holding her hand. "It's okay, Gram, to admit you're a little nervous about surgery."

The older woman grinned at her. "All right, I am having some nervousness, and I'm aware that I'll hurt a lot when I come to. However, I've lived with constant pain since my fall, and that won't go away by itself. Once the surgery and the hurting are over—and the therapy—I expect to eventually get around fine."

Vanessa leaned over and kissed Gram's cheek, and didn't realize until Gram's arms came around her and the soft voice said, "Thank you, dear," that this was the first in a long time that she'd been the one to initiate such a loving embrace with her grandmother.

Why am I like this? Am I afraid to show love because Mother used to push me away when I wanted to hug or kiss her, saying she hated getting all rumpled? Almost with reluctance, she straightened. "Rob's put you on the prayer chain again."

"Tell him I appreciate his doing that. Why *should* I worry with all those prayers uplifting me?"

Vanessa admired Gram's being so bright-eyed and cheerful. "Do you have messages for the girls, or the family?" *That sounds as though I'm offering to dispense her final words—as though I don't think she'll survive!*

But before she'd figured how to make that sound better, Gram was saying, "Tell each of the girls how much I love her, just as she is now. And say that I also love her for what she *will* be, with God's help and guidance. I respect her for sticking by the decision to have her baby, and I'm looking forward to helping her through that—and afterward."

"Good morning, Gram!" Keith came strolling in, wearing a dark-blue business suit and tie. "And a good morning to you, also, Van."

"Are Andi and Katherine going home today?" Gram asked.

His eyes sparkled. "Leave it to you to think first of happy prospects, Gram! Yes, they'll be leaving later this morning, but right now they're doing something extra special." He stepped back a pace, his arm encircling his beautiful wife, who came in carrying a small, pink-wrapped bundle in her arms.

Andi looked indescribably happy. "Katherine and I got a special dispensation to leave our floor and come wish you the very best through surgery and recovery."

Gram had been tilted upward slightly and now, without thinking, attempted to sit upright and reach for the sleeping infant. She gasped, face contorted with agony. Sinking back against her pillow, she wiped moisture from her upper lip and forehead. "Thanks, Andi," she managed to say in an obvious struggle to keep her voice fairly normal. "How thoughtful and generous of you!"

"It's pure selfishness on my part." Andi was going along with Gram's facade of being all right. "We couldn't be in the same hospital and not come to be with you for at least a little while." She leaned over to kiss her and to settle her daughter in the arms of her great-grandmother.

It was just a short time before a nurse came with yet another presurgery form, and Keith and Andi left with the baby. Vanessa had planned to stay until Gram was actually on her way to surgery, but

Gram wouldn't hear of it. "As you see, I'm being very well taken care of. I appreciate your coming, dear, but you run along to your office, and get all those important things taken care of."

She didn't want to leave, but there were calls which should already have been made and a mix-up in Research and Development she hoped wouldn't be too difficult to straighten out. And she never knew what else could be awaiting her when she arrived.

While diligently working in her office at the plant, Vanessa received a call from her dad a little after two-thirty, letting her know that he was back from his business trip to Europe, and saying the surgery was over and Gram was in the recovery room, doing as well as could be expected.

She hated that expression; it meant so little! Was Gram as good as one would expect of someone her age, or good compared with everyone? And whose expectations did that refer to, anyway? Gram herself *expected* to be up and about quickly.

A shiver passed through her, there at the big desk in her pristinely organized office. Her own hopes had not been as high as they probably should be; Vanessa would never have Gram's kind of faith. She had, of course, participated in AnnaMae's prayer, and she'd been *hoping* a lot, but she didn't really know....

It was several more hours before Keith's call. "Hi, cousin!" he greeted her. "Good news—Gram was brought back to her room maybe an hour ago. She's having a lot of pain, but they say things went well."

"Great! About things going well, that is, not the pain. Are you still at the hospital?"

"I came home a few minutes ago. I'd brought Andi and Katherine here while Gram was in surgery, then had to go to the office for an hour or two, to take care of a rush matter. But I was there when they brought her back."

There were unfamiliar sounds in the background. "Am I hearing your little one?"

He chuckled. "Up until we started talking, Katherine was quiet as could be."

"I understand that happens when there's a child in the family, but didn't know they started *this* young."

"See? We knew she'd be precocious!"

Vanessa was only half joking when she suggested, "How could she help but be with you as her father?"

"Much *more* so with her one-in-a-million mother!"

There was a softness in the way he said that, and Vanessa thought that might be the whisper of a kiss she heard, and then an even softer sigh. She was almost jealous of such a love as theirs, which she was half-afraid to hope for...to one day experience....

Vanessa pulled in behind the big black sedan parked in front of Gram's house, wondering who was supplying dinner this time. She'd never been good at identifying vehicles and, besides, didn't know what cars her grandmother's friends drove. She seldom attended church except when she couldn't get out of a special invitation by Gram to an occasional Easter or Christmas service.

She heard laughter as she entered the hallway, and Rob's unmistakable deep voice. Gin Redding's higher-pitched one then said, "She'd have called if she was going to be real late, so you'd better wait to dish up till she gets here."

Vanessa was by now at the end of the hall, in the kitchen doorway. "It sounds as though I arrived just in time!"

They were all talking at once, then let Rob explain, "Mrs. Seaforth must have spent all day cooking and baking. She said she would prepare food if someone could deliver it, and I was the lucky one."

"Aggie Seaforth sent *all* this?" The table was covered with homemade cinnamon rolls and two pies in addition to numerous bowls and containers.

To the girls she added, "I thought she was old when I was a child." Then she turned to ask Gin, "What is she now? In her mideighties?"

The neighbor was near the back door, apparently ready to leave. "*Upper*-eighties, at least—but I'll bet she's had one great day of it! She had seven kids, you know, then all those grandchildren. It probably seemed like old times for her to cook for the six of you. Or more..."

"Stay and eat with us, Gin." Vanessa had walked over and was lifting lids. "There's so *much* here, and you know what an excellent cook our dear Agatha is."

"I don't want to butt in...."

"You *can't* butt in when you're invited, and the more the merrier, as Gram would say. You certainly deserve it, after coming over twice today.

"And you stay, too, Rob. After all, you brought all this."

Both protested only mildly before sitting down at the table. Gin gave thanks to God for the meal, and there was lively conversation as they ate. Everyone was relieved at the report of successful surgery, and optimistic about Gram's recovery.

Only once did anyone mention Rob's profession this time. He glanced toward Jana before replying, "I should get used to people wondering what kind of person chooses to become a mortician instead of a doctor or lawyer or automobile salesman or short-order cook. Y'know what happened when I first told Vanessa I'd decided to do this?''

She felt heat rising in her face and knew they must see her heightened coloring as he announced, "She *laughed* at me, that's what!''

He had never referred to that before, and she'd hoped he had forgotten. "That was incredibly rude of me," she admitted, looking at everyone except him, "but it was such a surprise. He'd talked for years of becoming a family practitioner or a physician's assistant, or perhaps a physical therapist. And for a while he even considered becoming a minister.

"Any of those would have meant intense involvement with *living* people, and then there he was, speaking of working with…" she stammered, unsure how to finish the thought without mentioning corpses or bodies "…with people after they've died." She forced herself to look at him and was relieved to see him smiling.

"It's okay, Van." His right hand seemed to be reaching toward her, but came to rest on the table's edge. "I shouldn't have teased about it."

Vanessa didn't know if Gin was deliberately maneuvering the conversation away from that topic when she told of two late-afternoon calls from people asking about Gram, but Vanessa was glad for the change of subject!

Rob soon explained that he had to leave, and she walked out with him and down the steps. "Thanks again for bringing Miz Aggie's wonderful meal."

His little nod was probably in place of saying *You're welcome,* but his words were, "Do you always call her that?"

She chuckled. "She was my Sunday School teacher when I was maybe five or six. Gram and other ladies her age called her by her first name, so I did, too, until Gram corrected me. But Mrs. Seaforth said I could call her *Miz Aggie*—well, that's what I understood, though she probably said, *Mrs.* Anyway, she's been that to me and many others ever since."

He stopped on the sidewalk. "She speaks very highly of you, Van, and is impressed with your moving right in here—taking care of the girls and everything."

"Gram's very concerned for them, and so am I. What's remarkable is that *other* people are doing so much."

He looked back toward the house. "I told Mrs. Redding that I could stay this afternoon until you got here, but she insisted she wanted to."

Her shoe scuffed against the leaf-strewn flagstones. "In order to get this facility up and running, a number of conditions had to be met, one being that at no time can there be unsupervised visiting by a male."

"I hadn't thought of myself as a 'visiting male.'" His mouth twisted into a smile. "But I can see that my motives could be suspect."

"Several times men or boys have called, wanting to visit or to go out with one of the girls, so it is a necessary rule." She grinned up at this man a good six inches taller than her height of five-eight. "There was no way of foreseeing that a nice, good-looking young mortician just might want to be helpful." *Is he wincing a little? It seems as though there's a flicker of—what?*

"I was already a man, Vanessa, even before becoming a funeral director—I was an individual before a professional." His words seemed more subdued than usual, and there was something like pain in his eyes. "I still am."

She glanced down at her shoe again, scraping back and forth in telltale discomfort. Transferring her weight to the offending foot, she looked back up into his deep-brown eyes, so near she could see herself in them. "I know."

Rob hoped she really did think of him as a man; his regard for her had nothing to do with her efficiency as manager and executive secretary of the plant started several years before by Andi and her electronics-genius father. He wanted to continue the conversation with some casual remark, but before he could do so she returned to the previous subject. "Miz Aggie must have been relieved at your willingness to bring the meal she fixed."

"It was my privilege. And I thank *you* for the invitation to stay for dinner."

"It was the least we could do. For both you and Gin."

Was she aware of his feelings and deliberately trying to remind him that it was not just he who'd been asked to stay? She started back toward the porch, but he noticed that she didn't go up the steps until he waved as he pulled away. She appeared to be moving more slowly than usual—could it be his wishing that made it seem so?

What did he really know of the Vanessa McHenry of today? She was so beautiful he could still hardly keep from staring at her, like he used to in senior high. That perfect, light-complexioned, heart-shaped face above the classic column of her neck; the long blond hair with just enough wave to emphasize its softness and catch the sunlight or moon-glow—or fashioned into French braids, as she sometimes wore it....

He drew in a deep breath and let it out slowly

as he turned into the alley, pushed the remote, and watched his garage door rise slowly. He drove in, got out of the car and started through the doorway into his house, almost forgetting to lower the door of the garage.

History does, indeed, repeat itself; you were so sure you could manage it this time—being a friend, just a helpful friend. But you never did get over her.

And you still have no idea what went wrong before, or how to keep it from happening again....

He went through the small utility room; everything was in order there and in the good-size kitchen. He'd promised himself that he would keep things neat when he bought this three-bedroom, ten-year-old brick ranch house.

He knew all too well from college days how easy it was to let things go. His room had always been in disarray and he was constantly searching for things. Well, he'd succeeded by sheer willpower in keeping *that* resolution; how could he now keep from falling even more deeply in love with this remarkable woman?

The sensible thing would be to keep a distance from her physically, but even considering that was painful.

Walking through the broad archway into the dining end of the large room stretching in front of the kitchen and one bedroom, Rob turned left into his office and pushed the answering machine's flashing button. The first message was from Elmer Harnish, his partner, asking him to call a son of the man whose viewing was scheduled for the next morning at ten, prior to the memorial service. The second was his mother, and the third had been left by Betty Jefferson.

There was no question as to which callback to make first, as he always enjoyed Mom's upbeat conversations. Several winters ago she'd been asked by Great-Aunt Beatrice Maroney to spend January and February with her in Fort Myers, on Florida's Gulf side. They got along so well that they repeated this every year, each time her stay getting longer.

Physically better there, Aunt Bea decided to remain year-round. She was doing well, considering her ninety-two years, but diminishing eyesight meant she could no longer drive, and she wasn't surefooted enough to walk far by herself.

"We appreciate your letting us know about Gram's accident, and that she was going through surgery," Sylvia Corland told him. "We've been praying for her, of course, but do need an update."

He filled her in as much as possible, which led to her asking how Vanessa was making out with the five she, too, referred to as Gram's girls.

"It's been tough, Mom, so you might want to keep praying for Van. In addition to an extremely responsible load at work, she comes back at night and has to care for everything at her grandmother's."

"I'd think the girls would be able to go ahead with some things."

"I don't know for sure just what they're capable of. Women from the church began what I know you sometimes did—they're sending in the major meal of the day."

"Well, good! That at least takes off some of the pressure."

"But she's trying to do too much—helping the three oldest with preparations for GEDs, making sure the younger ones keep up with their homework, seeing that each one does her part with laundry, cleaning and other tasks...."

"Does she seem overwhelmed?"

"No, she doesn't, and I admire her for that."

There was the briefest of pauses. "Just go easy, dear."

He shouldn't be surprised, but hadn't expected her to sense his—love? Infatuation? "I took food for the first day, takeouts from the steak house." He chose not to mention staying to eat that night or the next one! "Aggie Seaforth prepared today's."

They spoke of a number of things, but near the end she came back to their initial topic. "When you see Gram or Vanessa again, tell them they're in our prayers. *All* of them are...."

The call to the deceased man's son took only a few minutes as Rob reassured him that someone would be directing traffic at each of the two major intersections on Broad Street, so cars in the slow funeral procession would not get separated.

Also, there'd probably be no difficulty adding another person who wished to share memories at the service, but this should be discussed with their pastor right away. And it was, of course, too late to have his name on the printed memorial folder.

He was smiling as he made the third call. Betty was four or five years younger than Vanessa and himself, twenty-five or twenty-six. He remembered her in Youth Fellowship during the last year or two before he left for college, a bubbly, outgoing, bright-eyed redhead involved with every program and service project.

She married Paul Jefferson soon after high school graduation, and they now had a four-year-old son, a two-year-old daughter and an infant. "Thanks for calling back," she greeted, "though you may be sorry you did."

He laughed. "I promise to at least give you the chance to tell about it before I hang up."

"I thought you might—hoped so, anyway. I was talking with Miz Aggie, and she said you delivered her dinner to Gram's. Right?"

He'd already guessed what she wanted and quickly offered to deliver the dinner she would prepare the following day.

He slowly set down the phone. His shoulders were straight and head high as he sat down in the tall-backed oak chair and glanced at the many cubicles in his antique rolltop desk. As good as he felt right now, he should be able to zip through the paperwork which had accumulated over the past two days. If only he could keep from thinking about Vanessa for just a little while....

Chapter Three

This night was not going nearly as well for Vanessa as she'd hoped. Oh, it started out fine, *more* than fine while Rob was there, but when she came in after seeing him off she found that neither Jana nor Barb had started her homework.

They sat glaring across the kitchen table, in a seething silence she tried to break by speaking directly to one, then the other. Receiving only monosyllabic answers to questions about their assignments, Vanessa leaned back in her chair. "Okay, who wants to tell me what's going on?"

Silence. Averted glances.

"Barb, please explain whatever I should know."

Jana pouted. "Just 'cause she's a few lousy months older, she always gets chosen first!"

"You were given the opportunity and could have answered. Now I'm asking Barb."

Barb was the quietest of the five, somewhat timid and nervous, the thumb of her right hand presently worrying a hangnail on her left forefinger. "Jana thinks she's the only person in the whole world!"

Vanessa shook her head, frowning, to stop Jana from interrupting. "Like with your friend," Barb continued. "Jana thinks Rob's falling for *her,* if you can believe anything that dumb!"

"He talked to me more than to you or anyone else! You *know* he did."

"'Cause you kept barging into every single conversation he tried to have! With Vanessa or Mrs. Redding or anyone."

"I was just being friendly!" Her dark-blue eyes were stormy. "Not like *you,* sitting there like some stupid old lump."

Jana's records had shown that she believed every man or boy who paid attention to her considered her irresistible. Although sexually active for at least two years, she was unwilling to take responsibility for being almost six months' pregnant.

"That's better than making an idiot of yourself and preening like a peacock. Or strutting your stuff."

"Oh, Miss Priss!"

"That is enough, Jana!" Vanessa turned back to Barb. "Is there anything you want to add?"

She drew in a quick breath and opened her mouth, then closed it again as she sat there in thin-lipped dudgeon. It was several seconds before she blurted, "She's always running me down!"

Vanessa knew Barb needed building up, but she couldn't do that now. "I know how hard it is for both of you, being seventeen. I had a rough time of it, too, when I was your age. But Gram's doing everything she can to help all of you through this, not only because of your age but because you're pregnant, which also can make women edgy.

"It's been a tall order right from the beginning, but she's done her best, and at this point we don't even know if she can continue it when she gets out, so..."

Barb was leaning forward, staring. "You mean—we might get sent back *home?*"

That last word came out as a high-pitched squeal, and the girl's hazel eyes were so huge Vanessa could see white all around the pupils.

"How would you feel if that happens?"

"I'm *not* going back there." Her head moved forcefully from side to side. "No one can make me do that."

"Then it behooves you and Jana to shape up."

"I mean it. I *won't* go back." Barb never looked well, as skinny as she was and often, like now, her head and shoulders were bent forward as though carrying a tremendous burden. "I'll run away first—or kill myself."

She's seldom this forceful, this dramatic, Vanessa thought. "*Was* it that bad?"

"Worse!" Barb's hands were wringing one another there on the table. "Mom picks such *awful* guys!"

Vanessa couldn't remember the reports going deeply into the lifestyle of her mother, but as she was trying to decide how to ask the question, Jana burst out with it, "Is *he* the guy who got you pregnant?"

A shudder ran through Barb. "I don't even want to talk about him. He's evil!"

What would Gram do? Vanessa wondered. Would she keep the girl talking, hoping that, once out in the open, it could be dealt with?

Jana was already asking, "Did your mom know about it?"

"She didn't do *anything*. She's as bad as he is!"

"*Worse,* if you ask me! My mom didn't give a hoot about me, but I can hardly believe yours would let her boyfriend do whatever he wanted! *Both* of them should rot in jail."

It's amazing—Jana's utterly appalled by the

wickedness done to this girl she herself harasses!
But what Vanessa said was, "At least you're safe
here, Barb."

"I'm—not sure. Mom had to sign for me to
come, since I'm just seventeen, so she knows
where I am." She fidgeted as she cleared her
throat. "Two days ago a red car went past here
that *looked* like his. But I ducked down, so I can't
say absolutely, positively it was him driving, but
the car had a replacement fender on the right front,
just like his. And it was going real slow."

Vanessa tried to keep from showing her horror
at this development. "Have you told anyone?"

Barb's long, straight blond hair whipped from
side to side with her vigorous head shake. "I
thought I'd tell Gram yesterday, but am sure glad
I didn't!"

"Glad?" Jana challenged, eyes still large.

"If she'd fallen right after I told her, I'd *never*
have forgiven myself!" Her hair swung forward,
partially concealing the tear-smudged, downward-
tilted face.

Vanessa went to her, reassuring, "We understand your being frightened, dear, but I'm glad you
told us. We can help you."

"Nobody can—not forever." It was a wail of
hopelessness. "He could grab me on my way to
school. Or come here…"

"I don't think he'd try that—not with all of us here with you."

Jana chimed in with her own encouragement, "Sure, we'll tell the others and—"

"Don't tell *anyone*. I shouldn't have said anything. I didn't plan to."

"We had to know, Barb. From now on I'll drive you to school each morning, and you two can make a point of coming home together." Aware of Jana's apprehension, she asked, "You often walk back with other girls, don't you?"

"Just sometimes." Barb looked toward Jana. "And I don't want you or anyone else hurt."

Vanessa needed to ask, "You honestly think there could be danger to others?"

"I don't know. But I've been so scared...."

Vanessa worked hard at helping with homework, but they had difficulty concentrating. It was after the girls had gone upstairs, and after she'd spent another hour working with the older girls' studies that she checked a second time to make sure all first-floor doors and windows were locked. She considered pulling the opaque shades at the kitchen windows, but couldn't recall Gram's doing that except when midsummer's late-afternoon sunshine streamed in.

She did, however, deliberately leave on both back and front porch lights, and was going back to the kitchen when Rob phoned to tell her of his mother's prayers. He added, "Honestly, Van, I don't know how you're doing everything!"

"The question isn't so much *how* I'm doing, as how *well*." She'd tried to say that lightly, but surprised herself with, "I wish Gram were here!"

There was a split second's pause. "What's wrong, Vanessa? Is it something I can help with?"

His voice sounded worried, and she wanted nothing more than to share this with him. "I shouldn't...."

"Van?"

"It's, not something I can talk about on the phone." *Actually, I shouldn't talk about it at all.*

He must have sensed her turmoil. "I'll be there within three minutes."

She felt guilty involving him in this, and told herself she should be calling her lawyer-mother for advice. Instead, she went out on the front porch and sat on the swing for what proved to be no more than the short time he'd predicted.

She'd told herself she had no right to trouble him, but as he parked along the curb, hurried up the walk and steps and then across the porch to sit beside her, she knew she needed his input and suggestions, and felt heartened by his presence.

He held her hand as she filled him in on Barb's situation, and how worried she was. He asked questions, most of which she couldn't answer, and talked about what-ifs and maybes—and it did help immeasurably just having him there.

They eventually went together into the house, Vanessa having decided to call her mother for advice. Rob used the phone in the front room; Vanessa sat near him using the portable phone, what Gram referred to as her "walk-around."

"Gram's not worse, is she?" Mother's concern was evident.

"She seems to be doing fine, but we have another problem...."

Paula McHenry said almost nothing as her daughter told what she'd just learned, but then she stated, "I'm calling the authorities tonight."

"Is there any other way? Barb's going to be terribly upset if this becomes public knowledge."

"We have no choice." There seemed to be sadness, at least resignation, in that voice. "Barb's a minor, and what's been perpetrated is a major crime which, by law, you and I *must* report."

"I doubt she'll be willing to repeat any of this."

"There are people specially trained to work with these situations. I think she'll open up once she finds this to be the only way she can ever feel safe." She cleared her throat. "The girls adore Gram...*she'll* be able to get Barb's cooperation."

Rob, too, asked Paula questions and discussed

the situation with her and, later, with Vanessa, leaving only when she insisted she must get to bed if she was to be even functional the next day.

Vanessa had trouble sleeping, however, and awoke early. She must talk to Gram about Barb, and the sooner the better. She would have to find time today to run over to the hospital.

And then she stopped short, sitting there on the side of her bed, asking herself why she'd involved Rob with something that had nothing to do with him. *It was my own weakness, my own need. It's not his problem, and yet I dragged him into what could become very messy.*

That bothered her even after their neighbor came and Vanessa was driving the two girls to school. They were nearly there when she told them what her mother had said.

"He'll *kill* me!" Barb had become almost hysterical. "He said he would—over and over he said he'd kill me if I told anyone! And he'd kill *Mom*, too. I *trusted* you, Vanessa, and you've already told someone else!"

They were still a block from school, so Vanessa pulled to the curb, stopped, and turned to look her in the eye. "My mother is our legal advisor, the one who took care of all those forms and regulations that made it possible for Gram to open her home to you. I *had* to touch base with her, Barb, for your sake and for everyone else's.

"Gram, herself, would have to report this if she knew. Since I'm trying to take care of things while she's in the hospital, it was necessary to find out what must be done in order to stay within the law."

When Jana also started yelling about not keeping confidences, Vanessa stated firmly, "Listen, you two! We could be closed down if we don't obey the law. *Then* where would you be?

"Each one of you is more important to us than just keeping Gram's home open, but you saw a certain car, Barb, which could mean someone's looking for you, has perhaps found you. *Should* that be the case, the law is the only protection you have against what he could do."

"I can run away...."

"Where could you go where you'd be absolutely certain he can't find you?"

She almost mentioned that she and others could be hit with huge fines and lose the opportunity to continue doing for others what had been so recently begun, but that would seem of little importance to either girl right now. Instead, she tried to impress upon them the necessity of acting as normal as possible and staying together during lunch and after school.

She pulled up at the entrance nearest the cafeteria and pointed to the front corner of the parking area. "If at all possible, I'll be over there by the time school's out," she said. "If I'm not, wait *inside* these doors for another five minutes. If I still haven't come, walk back to Gram's—with others, if possible—and along the main streets."

They solemnly assured her they would do so, but as they left the car Vanessa added one more thing. "If you must walk home, go directly there." *I'm not sure that's strong enough.* "If you aren't home in a reasonable amount of time, we'll have to notify the authorities about two missing persons—which could become particularly sticky since we haven't told them what's going on."

Cars behind hers kept her from staying until the girls were inside, but she did check her rearview mirror as she slowly moved forward....

She tried to tell herself that this day was no worse than usual, but didn't believe it. Trouble with one packaging line right at the beginning of the shift kept that crew out of operation several hours.

A man in Shipping fell and hurt his back. The nurse didn't think his injuries serious, but recommended that for his own and the company's sake he should be taken to the hospital for X rays and evaluation.

It was then she learned that one huge carton of a large order of new-games-for-Christmas CD-ROMs had not arrived at a major wholesaler's, and their purchasing agent was threatening to cancel the entire order if this portion wasn't received by the following day. She finally got him to agree to giving them *two* days, but finding what went wrong and getting that taken care of took far too much of her time and attention.

She was out of her office more than usual, leaving Suzan Gibson, her secretary, to handle problems with her usual calm efficiency. Except for a granola bar and coffee, Vanessa had eaten nothing since a small breakfast, but was at her desk finishing a report that had to get out today when Suz came in. "You need an apple break, boss-lady."

Leaning back in her chair, Vanessa reached for the shiny Red Delicious apple that Suz offered to her. "Ummm, it looks wonderful." Shifting position and stretching, she glanced at the dainty ormolu clock Gram gave her when she first assumed the position. "Oh, no! It's nearly four!"

"What's that about time flying when you're having fun?"

She ignored that remark as she struck her forehead lightly with the palm of her hand. "I intended to pick up the kids at school."

Suz was shaking her head as she started for the

outer office. "In case you hadn't noticed, Vanessa, they're in high school now. How 'bout giving that mother-hen complex a rest? Haven't they walked home most days?"

She tried to smile, to come up with anything but her real reason for fretting, but blurted out, "It's impossible for me to take Gram's place in their lives!"

"Be yourself, Van." Suz turned back to face her. "They don't need cookie cutter adults around them, they need authentic, honest-to-goodness real people who care."

"I'll try to keep reminding myself of that." *Will they believe I care?* she wondered. *If only I'd paid attention to the time and got to the school when I said I would—but then I'd have had to come back later.*

She reached for the phone as Suz closed the door after herself. Gin answered, saying that Jana and Barb were at the kitchen table doing homework. "Tell them I got held up here, but hope to be home by five-thirty."

"Okay—and I understand it's that dear Betty Jefferson preparing today's meal. Maybe you'll be here when she comes."

"I'll try to be." It occurred to her that thus far the food had been provided by people she would least have expected. *I consider myself a good judge of character, but these folks from First Church are amazing....*

Little Teddy Jefferson came running across the yard as Rob's car stopped in the driveway. "I been waitin' and *waitin'* for you to come."

Rob got out and stooped to pick up the child, toss him in the air, then catch and set him on his shoulder. "I've been waiting for that, too, my young friend. Let's go inside and see what your mama and sister and baby brother are doing."

"Yeah!" He bounced a little more than was warranted by Rob's long strides. "Mama's been bakin' and cookin' all day long, and I've been a'helpin'."

Rob grinned, surmising that cooking help from a four-year-old would not make work easier.

Betty held the door open for them while, with her free arm, she scooped up the two-year-old trying to get outside. "This isn't too much of an inconvenience, is it?"

"I'm not the best cook in the world, Betty, but I do drive. This way we pool our strengths."

She smiled up at him, probably not realizing he'd provided the first meal. "I love cooking, and it's little more time- or energy-consuming to make double of everything. So," she continued with a sweeping gesture toward countertops covered with food, "our dinner and theirs came out at the same time."

"Wow! Even pineapple upside-down cake for dessert!"

"It's Paul's favorite, and I don't make it as often as I should. He'll enjoy some when he gets home tonight."

It took two trips for Rob to get everything to his car, and he was just starting up the front walk at Gram's with his first armload when Vanessa pulled up. "You're getting enough practice as a delivery-man to hang out your shingle," she greeted, walking toward him as he waited. "If you need a reference, I'm available."

It's not as a reference I wish you were available! But he had no right to think such a thing—was almost shocked that he had. "Miz Aggie beat you to it, for she's the one who told Betty. It's a lot easier for me to bring this than for her, with her three little ones, especially since the baby has an ear infection."

She nodded, then glanced back toward the car. "Is there more?"

"Mm-hmmm, but I'll come back for it."

"Don't be ridiculous. All I have to carry is this," she said, raising her calfskin attaché case a few inches.

"Okay, you asked for it." He handed her the box he'd been carrying. "I'll bring the hot things."

He'd expected her to go on, but was inordinately pleased when she waited for him to pick up the even larger, towel-covered box and push the car door shut with his hip. He came back toward her, going slowly enough to enjoy watching as she gracefully walked up the steps in front of him.

Kate met them at the door, offering to take part of the load, but Vanessa shook her head. "Things are well balanced weight-wise, and might shift if anything's removed."

"Rob?"

"No, thanks. This is more bulky than heavy."

Jana and Ricki came running down the wide, carpeted stairs, so everyone was soon in the kitchen. Vanessa placed a hand on Mrs. Redding's shoulder as she picked up her sweater. "Stay and eat with us, Gin."

"That's not necessary, dear. Really." She took another step toward the back door. "I'm glad to help out...you don't need to feed me."

"Of course you'll stay. We enjoyed having you and Rob with us before, and want very much for you to do it again."

Gin looked at him with uncertainty, so for her sake as much as his—at least he told himself that—

he grinned at her, then Vanessa. "You've talked us into it."

This could become addictive, he told himself later, as the conversations swirled around him. Then he pulled himself up short, both physically, by sitting straighter in his chair, and psychologically. He'd been talking a lot, but now paid more attention to everyone else at the table.

Gin said Gram called late in the afternoon to report that the therapists not only had her out of bed, but took her by wheelchair to Rehab, where they had her try to walk with the parallel bars.

AnnaMae looked appalled. "How did she make out?"

"She said it was awful!" Gin made a face. "She tried real hard, but only managed a few steps. She hopes it will go better tomorrow."

They talked about that, then about various things Phyl Bastian had discussed with the older three that day. Jana, who'd chattered most of the time the previous evening, said very little, and Barb was noticeably silent, toying with her food but eating little, and not looking anyone in the eye.

Vanessa must have noticed, too, for several times Rob saw her throwing worried, or at least concerned glances in that direction. She asked no questions, but when the phone rang as they were eating dessert, he thought that Barb's expression betrayed panic as Vanessa left the table.

She relaxed with Vanessa's first words, "Hi, Keith, how's that wonderful baby and her mom?" She was smiling at his answer and said she was pleased Katherine slept six hours during the night. Then, her back to those at the table, her voice became lower, words indistinct.

Everyone was *too* quiet, so he asked Gin about someone at church, and tried to draw the girls into conversation. Vanessa, coming back to her seat, said Keith had gone in to see Gram for a short visit, and from there the talk drifted naturally in other directions.

Gin finally said she must go, which seemed his cue to leave also.

Barb had not said a word.

Vanessa checked homework while the rest of them cleared away things from dinner. She didn't feel like working on GED material, so was relieved to learn that Aunt Phyl had done some of it with them in the late morning. She agreed with Ricki's suggestion that if they got through the next three pages, then into pajamas and robes in time, they could join the younger two for a TV special. After all, it was Friday—and apparently Gram permitted them to sleep in Saturday mornings.

While the girls watched TV, Vanessa phoned her parents' house to speak to her mother about Barb. Her father usually wasn't the one to answer when she called, but this time he seemed cheerful and talkative, so she spent four or five minutes with him before asking to talk with her mother. Paula stated that preliminary notifications had been made to the authorities, and she was hoping for some sort of response soon.

Paula had kept copies of all studies and reports, so she had the names and address of Barb's mother and her live-in lover, as well as employers and activities. There was also a little information concerning Barb's older sister, who had run away several years earlier, but Paula had no way of knowing if she, too, had been molested.

Vanessa took the phone with her when deciding to relax in a long, soaking bath, but after receiving three calls from Gram's friends and one from work, she left the line open. She rarely had opportunity to read just for pleasure or relaxation anymore, so enjoyed lying back in the old-fashioned, comfortably slanted, claw-footed tub to peruse several *National Geographic* articles.

Finally going downstairs in her robe, she divided the rest of the upside-down cake for them to enjoy as they watched the end of the show. After the girls trooped upstairs, she checked that all the doors and windows were locked.

No one seemed to notice that the porch lights were again left on.

Chapter Four

Vanessa had appreciated the offer from Aunt Shelby, mother of Keith and Karlyn, to come this Saturday morning to stay with the girls so Vanessa could visit the hospital. "I'm sorry I haven't got to see you since your surgery," she apologized, entering the sunlit room.

Gram, sitting in her wheelchair, stated firmly, "*You* are the one who's kept my sanity through all this."

Vanessa glanced around as though wondering to whom her grandmother was speaking. "You can't mean *me*...."

"I most certainly do." She wheeled herself close enough to reach out for her granddaughter's hand. "You have no idea how often I've thanked God for you!"

Tears were dangerously close as Vanessa leaned over to hug Gram. "I'm trying, but I'm not doing very well at managing all those things you do."

"How *could* you, with everything else you must take care of? And I have yet to hear one word of complaint."

They spoke of Gram's therapy and of the girls' studies, of Gin and Aggie and Betty. Gram was the one to bring up the subject of Rob. "What a fine young man he is. Everyone likes and respects him. I presume you know that he's already been elected to the church's Board of Deacons?"

"Perhaps that's why Miz Aggie and Betty felt so free in asking him to deliver their food."

"Wouldn't be one bit surprised." She pointed toward the riot of orange, bronze and yellow mums in a huge, gold-foil-wrapped vase. "They were here when I got back to my room after surgery. Gin and the girls picked them from my own garden, thinking I'd enjoy the autumn colors, and Rob delivered them."

"They're beautiful." She cleared her throat. "No one said a word about doing that."

"I forgot to mention it to you on the phone, though I did thank them. I sometimes do that—tell one person the same thing several times and neglect to mention it to others. And we *have* had other things to talk about.''

Although she wanted desperately to have input and prayers from Gram right now, Vanessa made the deliberate decision not to mention Barb's situation. Gram didn't need additional worries right now.

Vanessa stopped at the supermarket on her way back from the hospital, remembering they were almost out of milk, laundry detergent and other things, as well. She was getting the two bags from her car as Aunt Shelby came out, saying she needed to get home right away, but would be available to help the next day if needed.

Vanessa drew in a deep fortifying breath as she went inside, readying herself for the questions the girls would ask about Gram. It was a minute or two before she asked, ''Where's Barb?''

''In her room!'' Ricki was obviously annoyed. ''She's been sulking all day! I was up a while ago and asked why she was in bed. She *says* she doesn't feel good.''

''Well, I'm going up to change clothes in a few minutes, so I'll look in on her.'' What would Gram say or do? she wondered. Perhaps I should have talked this over with her, for I sure don't know how to handle things!

Checking dishes of leftovers in the refrigerator,

she found a variety of meats, pastas and vegetables to heat in the microwave. "We might as well finish some of these for lunch. I doubt that meals will be brought on the weekend, so we'll send out for pizza this evening."

"Vanessa?" Kate asked somewhat hesitantly after eating, "I make a really good spaghetti sauce, and we have pasta on hand, and you've brought hamburger."

"Great! Do you need other ingredients?"

"Gram's always got onions and garlic and seasonings."

"I appreciate your offer. I've got papers from the office to go over, so I'll count on your being in charge of not only organizing things for lunch, but of preparing dinner too."

But the church organist called right after that to check on when to bring *her* contribution of roasted chicken dinners already ordered from a Sylvan Falls church's annual moneymaker. Vanessa told Kate of the change and assured her, "I know we'd have loved your meal."

"Hey, it's okay with me. I'll make spaghetti another time." She shrugged. "I was just trying to do my part—but sometimes it's better to let others have the joy of helping."

Vanessa's smile developed thoughtfully. "You are a very wise young woman. It takes some of us a long time to recognize and accept that." That's probably why I was so pleased at your offering to cook.

When she'd checked before lunch Barb appeared to be sleeping, but when she went back upstairs, Barb was lying there crying. "I sh-shouldn't have told you that last night! I'm sorry."

Vanessa sat on the side of her bed. "Was it the truth, Barb?"

She nodded. "But I s-still shouldn't have said it—and I'm so *scared*." She rolled onto her back. "He said he'd kill me if I told. And kill Mom, too...."

It was then Ricki shouted up the stairs, "Hey, you guys, Andi's here, with Baby Katherine!"

Barb dried her eyes as she got out of bed, and walked with Vanessa to the bottom of the stairs. AnnaMae was already seated on the couch, holding the infant on her legs so she, as well as Kate and Jana, sitting on either side, could look down into and caress the delicate little face and hands.

"Oh, Andi, she's so *beautiful*, a perfect little doll."

Barb dropped to her knees in front of them, a look of wonder on her face as she gazed at the infant. There were tears in her eyes as she murmured, "It must be wonderful to have your baby, and for your baby to have a daddy, as well as you, her mother.''

Andi placed her hand on Barb's rumpled hair. ''It's even more wonderful than I anticipated, dear.''

Barb looked up at the poised, beautiful woman she'd known only since coming to Gram's. ''Andi, would you—*could* you ever give her up?''

''That's too awful to think about.''

Vanessa's heart sank; these girls had agreed that their infants would be adopted! She started to say something, but Andi must have realized where this conversation was heading. ''Keith and I knew before we married that we wanted children, so we worked on our house and made plans.

''It was sort of like birds making the nest ready for their brood, or lions preparing a cave or hole for their young. But this is so much better, for my husband and I worked together, consciously making arrangements and preparations.

''We even planned for the time when this should take place—and God answered our prayers in a marvelous way, with our blessed Katherine.''

''But don't you think,'' Ricki asked, ''that *we* can love our babies just as much?''

Vanessa was grateful it was Andi who was being asked, and replying, ''Yes, Ricki, I do believe that.'' The new mother sat down in the low rocker in front of them. "From what I've seen, I'm sure you could, but that's not the only question that needs an answer.

"The other is equally important, perhaps more so, and I respect each of you *immensely* for having the courage and strength to have asked what's best for your baby, and to act upon that. It would have been so much simpler for you to take the easy way out—to have the abortion your parents or the men in, or *out,* of your lives wanted."

The baby started squirming, her little face wrinkling and mouth opening wide as she began to cry. AnnaMae's hands slid under her, lifting Katherine up against her shoulder.

She's been around babies, Vanessa realized. The ease with which she handles Katherine, the way she's sort of rocking from side to side....

For just a moment she felt envious of her cousin's family. Andi had everything—wealth, beauty, a nice home, a loving husband and now this adorable baby.

She tried to force such thoughts from her mind, to follow the conversation which was turning to relatively inconsequential topics.

Keith walked over some time later, and was the one to carry their sleeping infant back to their home.

All six of the women had trooped out onto the

porch when they left. Vanessa sensed sadness in their hearts as they must be contrasting their own lives with that of the contented couple walking hand in hand down the sidewalk.

She sucked in a deep breath before asking briskly, "Is each of you finished with Saturday duties?"

Jana admitted, "I didn't get the porches and walks swept yet, but I will." True to her word, she was soon out again, broom in hand.

"I'm going inside before I'm swept away, along with the leaves and dust," Vanessa teased the girl sweeping with such gusto. "And if anyone else has forgotten her must-be-done-before-Saturday-night assignment, you know to check the list on the refrigerator door."

She turned just inside. "Call me when dinner arrives. Until then I'll be in my room, busy with that never-ending office work." It had been impossible since Gram's fall to stay late at the plant when things piled up.

She was so engrossed she could hardly believe it was after five when AnnaMae said Mrs. Ammand was there. She hurried down to greet the tall, thin, middle-aged woman who played the church organ so beautifully. "Thanks, Lucy. It's wonderful of you to bring all this." The sweep of her hand encompassed six large, compartmentalized foam boxes, as well as a chocolate cake and a container of salad.

Lucy lifted one of the lids, revealing a perfectly browned chicken leg and thigh, along with scalloped potatoes and peas. "I didn't ask whether you prefer light or dark meat, so there are three of each."

A couple of the girls stated preferences, but Vanessa reassured, "This is great, Lucy. Perfect. We're going to sit down and eat right away. Can you join us?"

She shook her head. "Thanks, but I ate mine when going to pick these up. I'm now on my way to the church, for I want to go over the music for tomorrow's service one more time."

The prayer had already been said, by Kate this time, when Ricki murmured, "I miss Rob's not eating with us. He's such a friendly guy."

Vanessa had been thinking the same thing, but wouldn't have expressed it. Jana interjected, "He couldn't come—he's the one on call at the funeral home for the weekend, and had to go pick up a body."

Vanessa lowered her chicken leg and stared at Jana. "How do you know that?"

"Oh, I called when I thought Kate was making spaghetti. Rob said he appreciated the invitation, though."

She didn't want to reprimand the girl publicly, yet had to explain, "I know you enjoy having him with us, Jana, just as we all do, but in the future it's best to check with me, or Gram or whoever is here."

"I didn't do anything wrong!" she defended. "I just said if he was free, he could come."

"I understand. However, I'm asking that none of you take Gram's hospitality upon yourself."

That made no sense whatsoever to Jana, since Vanessa had invited him before, but she reluctantly agreed to ask before doing anything like that again.

Rob parked the hearse in the area near the receiving dock and walked into the hospital's main desk area. He was told the body he had been sent to pick up was not ready yet. No one could give an estimate as to when he should come back, so he returned to the huge brick house that had been so carefully adapted into a funeral home that it retained its original mideighteen-hundreds elegance. As he drove into what had once been the carriage house for the wealthy lumber baron who'd lived here, Rob's partner, Elmer Harnish, came to meet him. "Problems?"

"Delays, at least."

The left corner of Elmer's mouth turned up in a rueful half smile. He'd gone through this far too many times. "So what are you going to do now—besides wait?"

"Might as well go home and kick off my shoes, maybe watch a football game or something."

But when he returned to his house at the far end of the block, he walked restlessly through the large living room and kitchen. He'd thought of making a sandwich and opening a can of soup, but he wasn't hungry. Not for food, anyway. Not primarily.

He remembered Jana's call just before he'd left for the hospital. Had Vanessa authorized her to invite him, or had she done it on her own? Although he considered her an impetuous child, he must remember she was a young woman, at least physically—as proved by her pregnancy. However, she still did have a markedly childlike attitude toward life.

He tried to call Ham Greever's widow to set up a time tonight or tomorrow morning when he could meet with her and get information for the obituary in tomorrow's paper. She either wasn't home or wasn't answering her phone.

He stood at the window, looking out over the street with its big old maple trees. It might be hours before he could claim the body, possibly not until morning. He glanced through the TV listings for the evening, but there was nothing he wanted to see.

What I really want is to see Vanessa, to be with her.

But if she'd wanted him to come, all she had to do was give him a call—give any indication at all. He had no right to read into her invitation to stay for the meals he himself brought as anything more than courtesy.

Going to the kitchen, he checked the refrigerator and cupboards. He had leftovers and a number of frozen dinners. He enjoyed preparing meals—but not just for himself. Not tonight.

He finally chose a Granny Smith apple from the refrigerator, washed it under the faucet, and carried it to the living room. Sitting down, he tilted the recliner back and slowly ate the fruit while reading the lead article in a newly arrived professional journal.

On Sunday, Vanessa almost groaned aloud as she opened one eye, looked at the bedside clock, and realized she should get up. Gram always took the girls to church with her, and would expect Vanessa to do so.

Well, it wouldn't hurt her to spend a Sunday morning in church for a change, she told herself, sitting up and bringing her legs over the side of the bed. A couple of the girls had not wanted to take showers last night, but she'd insisted; with the two bathrooms upstairs and the lavatory off the kitchen, even with the usual fussing with hair and makeup, it shouldn't take too long to get ready.

First Church was not overly formal, so she put on a blue cotton skirt and white silk blouse with an abstract dark-blue pattern the same shade as her eyes. A gold locket was the only jewelry she'd wear today.

AnnaMae came down in a dress that was undoubtedly expensive, and tight enough across the abdomen to leave no doubt as to her pregnancy. Barb, on the other hand, was wearing a very full cotton top to hide that fact, and it proved flattering, since she was so thin.

Two others soon followed, but as Vanessa turned to bring the platter of waffles to the table she happened to glance out the window. Barb was by the garage, picking an armload of flowers like the ones in Gram's hospital room.

"Those mums are gorgeous," Vanessa commended as Barb came in the back door and walked across the floor. "Do you know where Gram keeps her biggest vases?"

"Sure do." She carefully laid the tall flowers in the kitchen sink. "I'll get a couple from the butler's pantry."

Ricki grinned at Vanessa. "Imagine having your own butler, one needing a *pantry* even!"

Vanessa laughed. "I doubt that they ever had an official butler here, but there probably would have been at least a servant or two. However, that *was* the name given to the service room next to the kitchen."

"Go on and sit down," she told the other girls as Barb brought two tall, heavy, crockery vases to the sink. "We'll be with you in a few seconds, as soon as we put the flowers in water." They quickly arranged the flowers, and Vanessa took her seat where Gram always did, having considered it best to keep that already established place of authority. "Who wants to pray this morning?"

When no one answered right away, AnnaMae requested, "Would you, Vanessa, on this beautiful Sunday?"

She had not been asked since that first meal and now hoped to keep from betraying inner turmoil by more than that quick intake of breath. *Give me wisdom, God, and the right words,* was the heartfelt prayer she made preceding the one the girls would hear.

Reaching out to hold hands with Barb and AnnaMae, she bowed her head. "Dear Lord, thank You for this lovely day and for this food and for these wonderful girls around the table here in Gram's kitchen. Please take good care of them."

She squeezed Barb's hand, then AnnaMae's, before going on. "Please help Gram continue to steadily improve, so she can soon come back to us." *And that's not just so I can be freed from this responsibility, God.* "She's such a sweet and loving person, always doing so much for others, whether related to her by blood or friendship or need. Please free her from pain and heal her hip."

Now what? "And help us take care of things here, and make the right decisions, and be cooperative with one another. Give us the strength and courage we need each day, and the faith we need to get through whatever hurts and fears we have."

She should probably say something more. Oh, yes! "And help us get what You want us to from the preacher's sermon and what the Sunday School teachers have to say. Amen."

That wasn't as hard as she'd expected, but she was glad it was over! "Kate, help yourself to the waffles, then pass them, please. And I'd also like some orange juice."

Jana was pouring maple syrup over two waffles. "It must be nice for you—being a blood relative to Gram."

"Yes, it is." She nodded. "But my cousin, Keith, isn't, you know, and Gram couldn't love him more."

"I thought he was her grandson, and he married Andi, and that's how Katherine's her great-grandchild."

"I didn't know about that when I was small, but his dad died when he was real little and his widowed mother later married Gram's son. But I assure you that Keith is one of the *most*-loved members of our whole family."

AnnaMae's voice was softly thoughtful as she stated, "Then—Gram really does mean it when she says she loves us like family."

Vanessa's hand covered hers again. "Her heart is so big and her love's so strong that a little matter like whether we're biologically related doesn't matter at all."

"Everyone ready for church?" Keith's voice preceded him through the front door, the hallway and into the kitchen. "Want to join the three of us?"

Vanessa recognized the definite emphasis on *three,* and there was a chorus of yeses. She tried to be practical in replying, "We're ready, but planned to walk over since it's such a wonderful day."

"We're walking, too."

"Is Andi up to that?" she fretted. "It's only been a few days since the baby was born."

"Isn't she something?" A beaming smile covered his face. "Ask her why this is so important."

Jana got to the new mother first, asking the question. Andi glanced at Keith, then gave full attention to the others. "We definitely want church to be the first place we take Katherine, other than visiting Gram and you, that is.

"But as to walking, carrying our little one there, *that's* because we were reading the second chapter of Luke for our devotions the night before she was born. Remember Mary and Joseph taking Jesus to the Jerusalem Temple soon after His birth, to present Him before the Lord?

"Well, we know that was required of Jews for their first sons, but we decided to do it whether our child was a boy or girl. Mary *could* have ridden on a donkey but, since there's no mention of that even when they came all the way from Nazareth to Bethlehem, chances are they walked.

"So today we are walking the several blocks to First Church."

AnnaMae was beside her. "Then I guess you'd rather I didn't ask if I can carry her for a while."

"For this one time, AnnaMae, I'd like to keep her in my own arms."

AnnaMae nodded and offered a hopeful smile. "Maybe on the way back?"

"On the way home," Andi agreed.

Chapter Five

Rob was outside the church, greeting people and offering his arm to some who might welcome assistance. He was escorting Miz Aggie up the steps at the corner entrance when she came to a stop, looking down the street toward the center of Sylvan Falls. "Here comes Andi, carrying the baby, and Keith's with her! And Vanessa's brought her girls—and look at those flowers they're bringing!"

That was the first he'd heard them referred to as *Vanessa's* girls, which they were, right now. "I think I'll go meet them," he told her. "Perhaps I can carry one of those big arrangements."

"Go right ahead." She nudged him with her bony elbow. "I'm staying here, but you can carry those heavy flowers."

Her eyes seemed to be dancing as she looked up at him, and he wondered if she sensed how much he wanted to be with them—with Vanessa. He didn't see how she'd guess that, but didn't care if she had.

He met them halfway down the block, greeting the whole group with, "Isn't this a great day?" Clapping Keith on the back, he congratulated him and his wife on the addition to their family, then asked about carrying the bouquets.

Barb declined, since they were almost to the church, anyway, but Kate said, "Sure," and thrust her vase into his outstretched hands.

Was it by chance that he was walking beside Vanessa? He wasn't aware of consciously shifting position nor of her doing so, but she was asking, "Who died yesterday? Anyone I know?"

"Hamilton Greever, from over in the Crescent Creek area."

She frowned, as though trying to place that name, then gave a little shake of her head as he continued, "He and Sadie have lived for years in a small house at the foot of North Mountain. Other than a German shepherd, a hog or two, and a few chickens, it was apparently just Ham and Sadie."

"Sadie's his wife?"

He hesitated a moment. "I haven't had the chance to meet with her, to write the obituary. But they've lived there for at least fifteen or twenty years.''

Rob was starting up the three outside steps when Barb touched his sleeve. "*Now* you can carry these."

His first reaction was to say they could both walk up the aisle to place them on the marble-topped stands on either side of the pulpit, but instead he reached for it. Both of the arrangements were bulky, and her vase was too large for his hand to encircle. "Am I allowed to rescind my offer, Barb? My shirt's going to be thoroughly water-sloshed if I hold these against myself."

Her head tilted to the side before she slowly nodded. "I'll follow you, but you set them where they should be."

"We'll be partners on this project." He grinned at her, then the others. "And we'll meet the rest of you downstairs for Sunday School."

"Fine. We're going in the side door to the lower level." Keith started around the corner with the others. "No point in Andi's going up these steps, through the sanctuary, then back down again."

Even though Rob talked to Barb and gave her plenty of opportunity to respond, she said almost nothing until they were going down to the lower level. "I wish I was in Karlyn's group with you and Vanessa," she told him. "I feel sorta out of place with the high school kids, even if that *is* my age group.''

He almost said he was sure it would be all right but stopped himself in time. Gram was the one to make decisions like this, and she'd placed the girl in the other class. ''You know all of them by now.''

''But they already had each other to be friends with. And sometimes they talk behind their hands and look at me funny. *They* know I don't belong.''

''But you *do,* Barb.'' His hand reached out to touch her arm, but he saw her pull back, saw what looked almost like fear on her face. Even while drawing his hand away until it was safely in his pocket, he wondered what he'd done to make her afraid. ''Gram's one of the most respected and best loved members of this church. If she brought you here and into that class, you most certainly do belong!''

''It's not that simple,'' she murmured. ''I'm the *odd* one, the one with no family.''

''We'd like to be your family. All of us would like that. And to Gram and Vanessa, you're *already* family.''

There was a pooling of unshed tears. ''I don't feel like I belong anywhere.''

They were at the bottom of the steps, and he knew she should go on to the classroom where the senior high students met. "Unfortunately, we can't always trust our feelings, Barb, even though all of us sometimes fall into that trap."

She looked distressed, but he continued with an illustration to his point, "Someone in my group might say something today that I could take as an insult, or as being unpleasant, even if it was meant as teasing or spoken with no intent to hurt. But I can't withdraw, or turn inside myself because of that. If I do, then others, not understanding my pain, may be hurt by my reaction."

Barb looked downward, toward his feet. "But everyone knows I'm here because I'm pregnant."

Rob reached out to lift her chin, smiling down at her. "As far as I'm concerned, Barb, you're one gutsy young woman—a *good* woman. I truly admire you for not just having an abortion, for seeing this through.

"And I also admire you for going outside this morning and bringing in those dew-covered flowers. I suspect you did that partly for Gram's sake, but it was also because you wanted to make God's house more beautiful.

"You have so much more going for you, my young friend, than you have any idea of right now." Several crystal drops started down her cheeks, and he was tempted to brush them away, but knew better. "Go on to your class," he said softly. "I will be praying for you...."

Sitting at the far side of the room, Vanessa saw Barb and Rob in conversation at the foot of the steps, saw the girl's tears, and Rob's hand tilt her head upward as he continued speaking. His beautiful smile made her slowly-sucked-in breath come haltingly.

"And here comes our late mortician!" one of the men sang out. "And he'll probably be even *later* by the time he gets his coffee."

Rob headed in that direction. "Right you are, Jeff, but this time I have an excuse—Barb and I have just made our sanctuary more beautiful by putting big bouquets of flowers on either side of the podium."

There were a few more joking comments before Karlyn started the class with prayer, including the giving of special thanks, "...for our very newest member, my niece, Katherine."

Karlyn was an excellent teacher, and got the entire group involved. Even Ricki, who started out sitting stiff and obviously ill at ease, eventually joined in.

The class was in the middle of a series called "I Want to See Jesus," and people had been given the assignment of looking for Him in their every-

day lives during the week. Vanessa was relieved
they weren't going around the room, asking for
examples, but was interested in what others were
saying.

Russ Collingswood told about some big, relatively new piece of farm equipment, which had
been down during the beginning of the week. He'd
mentioned to Jeff the countless hours spent in trying to get a necessary repair part. "And Jeff said
he was going to be in the company's home city on
Wednesday, and he'd check with me before leaving there, to see if it came," he related. "So he
did—and it hadn't! So my good buddy here
jumped in a cab and went right out to the company,
then flew back here that afternoon with the needed
part! How's *that* for seeing Christ in action?"

Andi said she experienced a new appreciation of
God's power and grace in the birth of her child.
"We talk about rebirth, and new birth, and being
born again, but I'm filled with awe when I look
into the face of our darling Katherine. Nine months
ago there were but two cells, which joined to become one entity which then divided and redivided,
each in its right sequence and time, just as God
ordained."

Vanessa saw AnnaMae's open hand against her
abdomen, circling a little, caressing the being
within her. *AnnaMae will not be able to give up*

her baby. She was as startled by that certainty as if she'd heard the words spoken, and even looked around the circle to see if that might have been so.

Other examples were given, but she said nothing, even when someone mentioned Gram's successful surgery, which reminded her of all the delicious meals which had been prepared for them.

It was Kate who told of Rob's providing the very first meal and delivering the next couple, but he shrugged off any credit. "What can I say? I'm a fairly decent driver, even if I've never won awards as a cook."

Vanessa bit her lower lip, keeping herself from speaking up, from telling how much she appreciated all he'd done and was doing—how she appreciated who he was....

Sitting along the outside aisle with three of the girls already with her in this next-to-the-last pew, Vanessa was pleased when Ricki walked only partway back the center aisle and sat with two other girls about her age. *I don't know if she's been doing this regularly, but I must remember to tell Gram.*

Jana nudged her as the choir came in, singing. "Doesn't Rob look cool in that long blue robe?"

"Yes, he does." She should have added that all the choir members did, but her eyes, like Jana's, stayed on the tall, brown-eyed, handsome man who was too rapidly becoming important in her thoughts—in her life. She watched him turn his head, as though quickly scanning the congregation. This happened again as soon as he was in the choir loft. Was it only in her imagination that his gaze met hers—that it stayed there—that those perfectly formed lips curved upward ever so slightly in a smile?

It was she who broke the contact, by looking down at her purse. I'm acting like a schoolgirl! she scolded herself—and hoped her foolishness was not noticeable.

Pastor Donald Harriman's message was about being joyful, at least contented, in whatever circumstances one found oneself. *How can You expect me to be joyful when I have no time to myself, when I'm so busy trying to keep caught up at work and seeing that things don't get any further behind at Gram's? I didn't ask for this, You know, and I'm doing my best, but I'm getting really tired— and less than joyful.*

Maybe it was easier to be "contented" in that time when the Bible was being written. But then the pastor stated that Paul was in chains and bound to a Roman guard at the time he wrote this injunction to the church at Philippi!

Well, there must be some other explanation then....

For lunch, they again ate leftovers—very good leftovers. Jana commented, "I hope no one comes while we're eating. With all these little containers and jars, this looks sorta strange."

"But there's no sense in emptying them into serving dishes." AnnaMae gave a crooked smile. "Especially when I'm the one scheduled to wash dishes!"

No one had changed clothes, for Vanessa had asked on the way home if they'd like to go with her to visit Gram. Things were cleared away quickly and all six were in her car and on the way within minutes. Vanessa felt a bit like the Pied Piper as she led them to the rehabilitation wing and they trooped into Gram's double room.

"Oh, my dears!" Gram exclaimed, her expressive face showing her pleasure. "It's so *good* to see all of you!"

"And it's wonderful seeing you sitting up in your chair to eat," Vanessa commended, but that was the last she got to say for some time. Each girl had things to share with this woman they loved, and they asked many questions.

Gram's roommate didn't have visitors, so Vanessa walked over to talk with her. It turned out that Vanessa knew her husband and son, both employed at the McHenry Division. Tom had worked there as a technician in Research and Development ever since the plant first opened, and their son had started his part-time job in maintenance as soon as he'd graduated from high school this spring.

"I understand Sam's working to help pay for his expenses at the technical institute," Vanessa stated.

"Mm-hmmm. He's living at home, but college is still *awfully* expensive. I wish he didn't have to work so hard, but that's the way things are."

She nodded. "Sam's a good worker, and dependable. Some of our very best employees are those who had to work the hardest to get the education and skills they'll use the rest of their lives."

"That's what we've told him, too."

Vanessa had been partially listening to the conversations of the others, and soon became aware that Barb, although sitting closest to Gram on the bed, was saying almost nothing.

Vanessa was delighted to see her father when he came in, and Gram reached out to him. "Brad! I'm so glad you're back from England. I was too groggy right after surgery to even ask if you had a good trip."

"Yes, I did." He bent to kiss her. "I wasn't due

to return until late tomorrow, but I made phone calls, and got to see a couple of contacts early— and here I am!''

He put his arm around Vanessa then, and she hugged him, too. "Have you seen the baby yet?"

"Sure did!" He grinned. "How about that? Keith a dad already!"

"He's plenty old enough, Brad," Gram reminded, "older than you were when you had your daughter."

There seemed a slight change in his expression, a tightening around his lips, but Vanessa decided she'd misread that, for his arm tightened around her and his lips touched her temple before he murmured, "And I'll always be grateful for her."

"And *I'll* always be grateful for all the time and attention you gave me as I was growing up, Dad." He looked startled, and she realized she'd probably never told him that, and should have. She explained to the girls, "Mother was so busy with her law practice that she didn't have time or energy left when she got home, but Dad used to take me with him wherever he went. And he went with me to all my school functions and things like that."

Into the momentary silence came Barb's softly spoken words. "I never knew my father. And my mother doesn't care."

Gram's hand clasped hers. "But *we* care, dear. We really do, very much...."

Vanessa chose to take the long way home—a *very* long way, as it turned out, for she drove along back roads through North Mountain, stopping at several overlooks.

"The last two or three weeks of October have always been my favorite time of year," she explained as they leaned on the strong, rustic-looking railing at the third one. "We're a little late coming up here on the mountain. The brighter yellows we see down in Sylvan Falls are already gone, but there is still a lot of the gold and orange and tangerine. And all these shades of reds and purples!

"Artists and photographers try, but there's no *way* of capturing this beauty on canvas, and no writer can adequately describe the feel of autumn."

AnnaMae had to give it a shot, however. "The sun is warm on my face and bare arms, yet the air itself is a little cool."

"Grandad used to call it *brisk.*" Vanessa had to consciously rein in that sense of loss at his no longer being able to come up here with her. And yet she clung to her memories of those many times throughout the seasons when she'd checked out this very site with that loving gentleman. But then there had been that awful fire at the mill in Sylvan

Falls and her grandfather, a volunteer fireman, gave his life in a futile effort to save a friend.

And now she was standing just about on top of this mountain, with five girls—young women!—who'd never been here before, to whom this was probably just a pretty view suitable for the October page of a bank's calendar!

Turning away from the steep, tree-covered mountainsides below her, she looked around at the parking lot where already, at 2:15, a number of cars were parked. She wasn't able to control her sigh before suggesting that they get home. "I have hours of business work awaiting me—but we did have to go to the hospital."

AnnaMae looked almost disappointed. "I thought you *wanted* to."

"I did! I wouldn't have missed that—nor our coming up here, all this beauty—all this *briskness*—and freedom. But now I must closet myself in my room at Gram's for the rest of the afternoon." But I wish I could stay here forever....

She was tempted to let the phone ring, to permit one of the girls to pick it up after the fourth invasive shrill, as she'd said they could. She was, however, nearly finished with what *had* to be done, so she reached for it. "Vanessa McHenry speaking. Can I help you?"

There was a parodied mournful voice saying, "Robert Corland here. And yes, you *can* help, by taking pity on a poor, lonely, hungry man. Would you let me borrow you and five other young ladies to get me over this condition?"

"Hello, Rob." She leaned back in her chair, even relaxing enough to lay her pen on top of the papers. "Somehow, I don't think of you as ever being lonely."

"Hey, I'm human—in case you hadn't noticed."

His voice had perked up considerably, and she allowed a small, audible laugh. "Oh, I've noticed, Robert Corland."

"Ah, you've noticed me. I take that as a very good sign."

"Well, we won't get into degrees of *good* right now."

"I guess it's okay to put that on hold—for now. But I was wondering about all of us having pizza together, or whatever might sound better."

Had his little sigh between those sentences been pure theatrics or could it have slipped out? "We've imposed on your time and generosity quite a bit of late, Rob."

"*Imposed?* That's definitely not the correct word! I've appreciated every moment with you."

He cleared his throat. "And now, as to that pizza?"

"Well...." This is ridiculous! I'm not usually so hesitant in making decisions, she scolded herself silently. "You mentioned all of us which, with you, is seven. Since that many don't fit in a car, were you thinking of our meeting somewhere?" But she was being presumptuous. "I'm sorry—you meant you'd bring it here, didn't you?"

"Actually, I had *not* meant that. I'd prefer going out, either to some smaller place like Raphael's or to one of the chains, whichever you or the girls prefer. And, as to driving wherever we go, would you or they be troubled by riding in the limousine? We'd fit in that."

"Why should that trouble us?"

"Oh, I don't know. It's big and black and shiny—and it may remind somebody too much of a funeral."

"Frankly, my friend, it doesn't remind me too much of gangsters or of royalty, either." And then she laughed. "The girls will be positively thrilled!"

"Great! So where shall we take them?"

"Since they'll be traveling in such luxury, what about somewhere more elegant than a pizza palace?"

"Sounds good to me. Do you have a place in mind?"

"Not really. This is a new idea. I was just playing with what-ifs."

"I like what-ifs." He sounded enthusiastic. "What about The Madison? Or the hotel's Susquehanna Room?"

"Either would be excellent!"

"Have a preference?"

"Not really—though I've been at the Susquehanna more recently."

"Then I'll call The Madison for reservations, and use the other for backup."

"Rob?"

"Vanessa?"

His tone was teasing, but she didn't acknowledge that. "I will, of course, share the cost for this."

"No, you won't. This is *my* treat."

"But you were inviting us for pizzas—I was the one who upped the ante."

"And I'm the one delighted to be the recipient of such excellent constructive advice." He may have heard her start to argue, for he quickly added, "Please don't take away my joy in escorting six lovely ladies to a classy restaurant."

"Well…" This didn't feel right, but she understood his position. "When you put it that way, how can I refuse?"

"How, indeed?" And then he informed her that, unless he called back within the next fifteen minutes, she was to assume things had worked out the way they wanted, and he'd be coming at six-fifteen.

Chapter Six

Jana, Kate and Ricki were back in what they
called their church clothes even before five-thirty,
Jana bemoaning that her pregnancy made her "as
fat as a cow."

Barb didn't even start changing out of her jeans
until shortly before Rob was to come, and
AnnaMae was later yet, still fastening the upper
button of her top while coming down the steps as
the others were welcoming him.

"Is everyone ready?" he asked. Receiving a
chorus of yeses, he smiled at Vanessa. "In that
case, let's go."

There was hushed conversation among the girls,
but Vanessa heard snatches:

"Wow! Look at that car!"

"Isn't that *cool?*"

"I feel like Cinderella!"

"Boy, am I glad I'm wearing something dressy!"

Vanessa sat in the front seat, with AnnaMae and Ricki taking the middle ones when the others scrambled into the back. "This rides like a dream," she murmured a little later.

He nodded. "Physical comfort's the least we can give those we serve."

"I suppose so." She looked toward him. "I've never been one of those riding in the limousine— for which I guess I should be thankful."

His glance met hers. "This *does* bother you."

Her head tilted toward the side as she considered that. "No, I don't think it does…. That was only a comment."

He looked forward, then back into her eyes, his hand reaching out to squeeze hers lying there on the small calfskin purse. "I'm glad."

His smile and gesture made her feel warm and cared for, as though maybe he meant to continue seeing her, perhaps take her in this luxurious vehicle again. She should respond, but didn't know what to say, then was saved from that necessity when AnnaMae murmured softly, "This is great— like the rest of this day has been!" And Vanessa told of their driving through the mountains after church, and how lovely everything was.

Rob parked the extralarge vehicle with practiced ease and they entered the huge old 1880s mansion, now converted into a restaurant. They were met in the front hallway by the epitome of an English butler, bowing and greeting them in subdued tones.

The man spoke to Rob by name and escorted them to a round table in the far corner of the huge room on the right, which she guessed must once have been a ballroom.

Tall potted plants gave some sense of privacy, but several people spoke to her, asking about Gram, and speaking of Keith and Andi's baby. Even more knew Rob, so there was probably some justification for Ricki's grinning at them after they were seated. "As well as you two are known, you couldn't get away with anything in this whole area!"

Rob laughed and, although Vanessa felt warmer than usual, she stated, "I'd rather not try!"

Their waitress came to ask what they'd like to drink, and then they were giving full attention to the menu. Rob said he was having the eight-ounce sirloin, and Vanessa wanted planked salmon, but the others spent time discussing various items and terms. It wasn't surprising when AnnaMae and

Jana finally decided on more unusual items, while the others chose conservatively.

AnnaMae had been looking at the centrally located, branched chandelier hanging from the ceiling. "Wow! That must have cost a fortune."

"By the time Pete and Janice Madison bought this place some years ago, *this,*" Rob's discreet hand movement indicated the whole room, which Vanessa estimated as at least twenty-five by forty feet, "was no more than a run-down apartment. He claims that the deciding factor in bringing the place back to its previous glory was their finding this ornate old gas fixture up in the attic, all tarnished and surrounded by lots of other stuff, most of which was of no use or value.

"So they tore out the dividing walls and the suspended ceiling, and found that wonderful plaster molding around the walls, eighteen inches down from the original white-plastered ceiling. And they were flabbergasted by that magnificent five-foot-in-diameter decoration in the center—so they had the light fixture electrified."

"Why would anyone cover up something this pretty?" Ricki wondered, twisting around to stare at it.

"There are a number of possibilities." He shrugged, indicating he didn't know which it might be. "This mansion was built by a lumber baron, but that business became no longer profitable after they'd clear-cut all the standing timber which originally covered most of this northern portion of Pennsylvania. And there had been devastating floods which demolished or severely damaged the mills and holding areas along the Susquehanna River.''

Rob glanced toward Vanessa, and she nodded agreement. She'd heard these stories ever since she was a child, from Grandad and Gram and from her own father. She enjoyed hearing them again, this time from Rob's lips.

He continued, ''I gather that his offspring and those of his former colleagues no longer did such extensive entertaining as before, so the changes to this room could have been made for their own kids or in-laws. Or they could have taken place even much later—perhaps some farmer fixed this for hired help....''

Their appetizers arrived, and the bowls of deliciously seasoned soup. The miniature homemade breads were good, also—and then came their meals!

What a fascinating way he has with the girls! Vanessa thought, enjoying the evening even more than anticipated. She'd subconsciously expected to be the one to draw out the teens, but Rob accomplished this skillfully, seeming to intuitively know what question to ask, what comment to make.

At least it worked for most of them, and, although Barb was still not talking much, those hazel eyes were taking in everything as they focused on whoever was speaking.

Several men and, later, a man and his wife crossed the room to speak with Rob, who seemed eager to introduce the members of his party. The first time this happened, several of the girls appeared uncomfortable, as though wishing no one to notice them. But they gained more confidence each time Rob introduced them as his good friends, with no mention made of Gram's taking them in because of their condition.

By the time a family group from church walked over near the end of the meal, even Barb and Ricki were prepared to speak with them.

Vanessa assumed that each was either consciously or unconsciously dawdling over dessert, not wanting this evening to end. It was she who finally looked at her watch. "Can you believe it's after nine already? We'll have to leave soon, Rob, for tomorrow's a school day and we have a busy week ahead of us!"

The girls protested, as she'd anticipated, but Rob smiled at her, then at each of them. "I'm honored to have had this much of your time and company, and have enjoyed every moment.''

She had no doubt the girls had, too, and they enthusiastically assured him of that.

''I hope we can do this again.'' And he added, ''Soon!''

That beautiful, enticing, open smile of his! Vanessa swallowed the lump in her throat before expressing her own gratitude in what she realized came out too formally. ''All of us appreciate your inviting us, and we've had a wonderful dinner and conversation. Thank you, Rob.''

Rob went with them up the walk and, without asking permission, followed them in as this remarkable woman asked the younger two to go upstairs immediately, saying that the others would come in five or ten minutes.

He had to consciously keep from showing amusement when Jana pouted about always being treated like a little kid, but Barb came to him, looking directly into his eyes. ''Thanks, Rob, for that real special dinner. And evening.''

''It was a pleasure—it truly was.'' He almost made a major error by reaching out to place his hand on her arm—which little gesture could have frightened her. ''You're a very special person, Barb.'' And it doesn't matter that I reused her own adjective! he thought. "I hope you'll stay in our area. I look forward to knowing the woman you're one day going to be."

Her eyes opened wide and lips tipped upward— but only for a moment. She glanced toward her feet, then at Vanessa and the others. "Good night, everyone."

He wondered if his emotions had been obvious, or if Vanessa just happened to touch his arm at that moment to reassure him, "If her mother's boyfriend doesn't create further problems, I think she's going to be all right."

The empathy in her concerned blue eyes almost unnerved him. His arms ached to hold her, and he suspected that, were they alone, nothing would keep him from putting them around her. But he couldn't do that, not here in the presence of the girls.

And not without having at least some idea of how Van really felt about him and how she'd respond!

He blinked hard to clear his vision and, hopefully, to clear his mind. Her head tilted in that questioning way he'd begun to recognize. "Headache, Rob?"

He grinned slightly. What would she say or do if I were to admit it was my heart, rather than my head, giving difficulties? he wondered. "I'm fine, Van—but thanks for asking."

Vanessa was out of her office the following morning when she was paged by her secretary. "One of your girls, Barb, is on line two, calling from a public phone off the main entrance at school. There's panic in her voice and manner, so I told her to stay on the line while I tracked you down."

Her heart pounded. Barb had never called her at work, so something was radically wrong. "Thanks, Suz. Yes, I'm glad you paged me."

She heard that familiar tiny click, indicating that the office connection was closed following Suz's saying, "Okay, Barb, here she is," then realized she was listening to the dial tone.

Barb was no longer there!

She checked back with Suz. "We lost her. Did she say what she wanted?"

"No—but she's one scared girl!" Suz was confirming her own worries. "Maybe she had to leave the phone."

"What did she say? Give me her exact words, if possible."

"Well—I think they were, 'I've got to talk to Vanessa. He's *here*. He was in the same car and...' Barb sorta stopped there for an instant before finishing, but then she said, 'And he tried to kill me.'"

"Oh, no!"

"I attempted to calm her, Van—but obviously didn't succeed very well."

"Did she indicate *how* he tried to do that?" Weak-kneed for a moment, she leaned up against one of the many cabinets in the office of the director of a new development project.

"She spoke of crossing the street at the edge of the school property, near the parking lot entrance. A red car came blasting out of there, right at her, and she said that if Jana hadn't yanked her between overgrown evergreens along the driveway, she'd be dead!"

"Dead?"

"That's what she said. Of course I don't know her, so I suppose she *could* have exaggerated...."

"She probably didn't!" But Vanessa couldn't go into that right now. "Look, do me a favor and call the school office. Tell them there's an emergency and I need to see Barb right away. Ask them to page her and say she's to come there right away."

She was standing erectly now, tense from seeing in her mind's eye how scared Barb must be. *Would she have stayed in the school? I can only hope she's still in the building! If not, where would she go? They each have a key, but would she risk being seen on her way back to Gram's?*

As soon as she got in her car, she used her cell phone to call her mother. If there was ever a time when she needed immediate legal advice, it was now! However, Mother's well-trained secretary stated that she was presently in the courtroom, where she'd probably be for at least a couple of hours, until the noon break.

"Would you see that she gets a message just as soon as possible? Tell her that Barb believes that a man in a red car made an attempt on her life this morning. I'm on my way to the school right now, and will probably have to give them some information—*especially* if what I got secondhand is correct.

"It sounds as though the vehicle came from on school property, and the incident itself probably took place on the street outside—in which case both the school and police will be involved."

Bernice Reilly, as coolly efficient as always, stated that her message would be delivered in the shortest time possible....

Vanessa picked up the phone from where she'd placed it on the seat beside her, then laid it back down. She had no right to infect others with her fears, her anxieties; Rob would probably come to be with her if she called, but she had no rights to his time or his presence. She'd acted out of her own weakness in getting him involved with this in the first place!

When she arrived at the school she had to park at the far end of the lot. Walking rapidly to the high school's front door didn't ease the fluttering of butterflies in her stomach. She'd seldom been here since her own graduation but, entering, she again smelled that indescribable mixture of floor wax, cleaning solutions and—and humanity?

She assumed the offices would still be where they'd been what seemed so very long ago, and they were, although there were now more of them, incorporating at least two adjoining classrooms.

She entered the door of the reception office, part of the totally glass-topped front of "The Portals of Death," as one of her friends who used to get in a lot of trouble called it. A bright-eyed woman looking no older than a student herself came to the chest-high divider. "Good morning, how may I help you?"

"I'm Vanessa McHenry, and my secretary recently called about one of your students, Barbara Mutchler." She gave a cursory glance around the room. "Is she here?"

An older woman who looked somewhat familiar had risen from her desk and, hand resting on the receptionist's arm, requested, "Please come around the end of the divider and follow me, Vanessa."

For just a moment, this seemed almost depressing—being told to follow someone into the school's inner office. But her immediate concerns pushed that from her mind. She wanted to demand more information immediately, but assumed Barb must be in the smaller room.

She was not.

"You may not remember me, Vanessa—I'm Nancy Foresman. I started as a guidance counselor near the end of your school years. I am now the assistant principal. I remember you."

"Being a McHenry in Sylvan Falls did make us stand out somewhat," she commented briefly, not wanting to get sidetracked. "Is Barbara Mutchler here?"

The well-manicured hand flipped outward, toward a chair. "Would you care to have a seat?"

"Not really. I just need to see Barb." *What was the big deal?* "Is she in one of the other offices?"

The woman remained standing, too. "We don't know where she is, either. Barbara did not go to her home room this morning, nor come to the office after the request over the PA system. And even though we got your message, we didn't want to make general inquiries until we knew if that was necessary. Do you suspect her of playing hooky?''

If only that were all I suspect! She shook her head, a certain grimness stealing over her. ''Please page Jana Jenson, then, and ask her to come.''

''Would you give me your reason for desiring this?'' she countered. ''We obviously can't continue calling people to the office.''

This had been said with a smile, but Vanessa was aware of the firmness behind it. Of course they needed more information. ''I was out of my office when Barb called, supposedly from a phone just inside your front doors. She was extremely upset, and told my secretary that someone in a car tried to run her down just as she got here this morning. She also mentioned that Jana was with her, and it was *her* quick actions which spared her life.''

Nancy Foresman reached for the phone and almost at once Vanessa heard the request over the speaker system that Jana come to the office.

It seemed like a long time, but the second hand had only circled the big wall clock's face twice when the door opened and Jana, looking frightened, was ushered in. Ms. Foresman closed the door behind her. ''Thanks for coming right away, Jana. It seems as though you're the only one who can give us some answers we need, so please sit here and tell Miss McHenry and me what happened this morning."

Jana sat on the edge of the indicated seat. Vanessa smiled as she, also, sat down, trying to remove some of Jana's fear or dread. "I wasn't in my office when Barb called."

Some of the tension left her face. "Oh, I'm glad she called! I said she should, but she kept saying she shouldn't bother you at work—that you needed all the time you have to get *your* work done, so you would have time for us."

Vanessa winced; she'd undoubtedly given that subliminal message, but would get that straightened out yet this evening! The girls had to feel free to contact her in case of real emergency. "Were just the two of you walking together this morning?"

She glanced toward the older woman, then at Vanessa, who added, "It's all right, dear. Just tell us what happened."

"Wel-l-l, like you said, we did walk here together, just the two of us. We'd been talking about a bunch of stuff—you know how that is and—and we'd just started to cross the street, where we always do...."

"Where *is* it that you cross?"

"*You* know, Vanessa, right where you drive into the school grounds when you drop us off." She fidgeted with a blouse button. "We usually walk on the far side of the street, 'cause there aren't as many kids over there...."

She must need encouragement. "Good thinking, Jana."

"A couple of guys behind us were arguing and talking loud, and I happened to look that way just as we stepped down onto the street. Barb screamed, 'It's *him*,' and started to turn, to get back up on the sidewalk. But she stumbled on the curb, so I grabbed her.

"And then I saw that red car coming right at us! I didn't have time to think—just shoved her real hard toward a break in Stanislaws' bushes, you know how raggedy they always are! And then I jumped back and started yelling, too."

The girl shuddered at the memory, and Vanessa saw Nancy busily jotting notes. That was good, since it would undoubtedly be distracting if she, herself, tried to do so. "What happened then, Jana?"

"Those guys, the ones who'd been talking so loud, were running toward us, and one threw a rock at the car...."

"Did he hit it?"

"Yeah, on the driver's side—the window!"

"Did it break?"

"Well, the glass didn't—uh—fall *apart*—but it

made that big spider-web sort of break—you know, the kind you can hardly see through.''

The other woman had still said nothing to Jana since inviting her into the room, and the chair Vanessa had chosen was off to the side, away from her. Hopefully, Jana wouldn't think about Nancy being here. ''Did you get a good look at the driver?''

Jana shook her head. ''Not much. I was too busy at first trying to save Barb and me, and then the glass was so crazy-cracked that I *couldn't*.''

There were many other things she should ask, but right now there was one major one: ''Where is Barb?''

Jana looked puzzled, then stricken. ''Isn't she here in school? I heard her paged.''

''She didn't show up at her home room. The last I know of her is that she called my office, supposedly from a phone right down the hall. By the time Suz paged and reached me, Barb's line was dead.'' *I wish I hadn't used that last word!*

''I tried to brush the worst of the leaves and dirt off both of us,'' Jana said, ''and we came inside together—along with a bunch of other kids. Barb was real shook up and started crying, and I didn't know what to do or say.

''But I *did* tell her she had to call you—and then I had to leave her there in the bathroom, cleaning up, 'cause the bell rang and I didn't want to be written up as late."

Vanessa drew in a big breath. "I haven't been able to get hold of my mother yet, but even though I can't, I think we have to go to the police."

"Oh, Barb'll be *real* upset."

"Granted—but we don't even know where she is. And if this man is who she thinks he is, and if he's now to the point of trying to kill her, then he's got to be stopped!"

She saw Nancy's eyes widen, and her mouth become an O, but she remained silent. "Going back to my question, Jana, do you have *any* idea where she could be?"

A shake of her head accompanied Jana's worried expression, but then she got an idea. "Remember that school shooting in New York, the one where a bunch of kids were killed? Well, we were talking about it then, and wondering what we'd do if it happened here.

"*She* said she'd head for the girls' lav, but I thought that would be too obvious. And then we mentioned cupboards, cabinets, lockers—especially those in the gym or library—or in the kitchen, if we happened to be in the cafeteria.

"But when we were coming in the same way as today, the doors of that big, deep closet that the custodians use—where they keep some sweepers and polishers and stuff, you know—was open. And I said if we were in the hallway when shots were fired, *that* might be a safe place to hide—sort of hunched down behind one of the machines...."

Vanessa restrained her desire to rush out and check those places, then figured that was what Ms. Foresman was doing when she slipped from the room. "Where else did either of you talk about?"

Her face screwed up with the effort to remember. "I can't think of anything."

"Okay, then. Do you think we could check the ones you mentioned?"

Chapter Seven

Rob had already put in quite a morning. There'd been that 2:00 a.m. call over at the Spruce Run Condominium, where a man had died. He hadn't really known Scott Listner although he'd helped the thirty-seven-year-old man make his own funeral plans eighteen months earlier. Scott had still looked fairly good then, which belied how he felt, but recently, down to less than ninety pounds, he'd requested a closed-casket service.

Rob had almost finished thoroughly cleaning the preparation room following the embalming when he'd received the call to go to the hospital's extended care facility for a ninety-five-year-old woman who'd been a resident there for over nine years. Jennie Bender, although totally blind since before she went into the facility, had been able to keep going, cheerfully, right up to the end. He and others on the church's transportation committee had enjoyed getting her on Sunday mornings, talking with her, and sitting beside her during services, realizing that she sang with enthusiasm every single word of every hymn!

"Why *wouldn't* I know them?" she'd retorted when he'd once commended her for her memory. "There are such meaningful words going with such beautiful music! You don't think I'd sing them without thinking about what I'm singing, do you? And, if I'm *thinking* about them, why shouldn't I remember them?"

"Why, indeed, Jennie." He'd laughed then, but now realized, with shame, that he didn't always think about the words he sang. For that matter, he couldn't remember right now what the hymns had been just yesterday!

Ah, Jennie, he thought, I will miss you, with your cheerfulness, goodness, and seeing the best in everyone. I have been blessed by knowing you....

But something had been bothering him since eight or eight-thirty—a nagging sense that something was terribly wrong. He'd blamed it on getting called out so early, and on the tragedy of Scott's last years. He was sure it had nothing to do with Jennie's dying, for this was what she'd prayed for:

"When the time's right, Lord, please just let me go to sleep here, and wake up with You in heaven."

The uneasy feeling did not go away. *What is it, God?* he prayed silently. *Is it something I should be doing? Something I've left undone?*

But still it lingered, frustratingly increasing instead of diminishing. *Is it something professional? I suppose that's possible, but don't have any idea what it is. If You'll show me, I'll try to do better.*

Is it at the church? Individuals in the church? Much of the mortuary cleanup duty was routine, so he often, like now, used the time while he worked to pray for specific needs.

Among those about whom he was especially concerned, Barbara Mutchler kept coming to mind. *She's so young to have to face these problems, God. She's trying to make a go of living here, of giving her baby its chance of life. Take care of her, Lord, please take care of her!*

He wondered at his own concern, knowing there were no romantic feelings involved, yet caring so much about her. It was almost as though she were his kid sister. *Is this what you mean by brotherly love, God? That I should feel as much for her as though I were her brother?*

But that raised different questions. Supposing

she *was* his sister, what would he have already tried to do for her—or wanted her to do for herself?

Well, for one thing, he'd want that boyfriend of her mother to pay the price for what he'd done to Barb. She was only sixteen when she got pregnant—after many previous rapes which her mother allowed! Yes, that woman should be punished along with her paramour!

Had Barb seen that man? If so, what was he after—and why had he waited this long to do anything, since Barb was sure her mother knew where she was? Was it possible that she had not given her lover this information until now?

He tried pondering this from all angles, considering even remote possibilities. His conclusion was that the most likely scenario for the man's actions had many parts. First of all, Barb was having his child and planned to put it up for adoption—but what if she decided at the last moment to keep the child and to sue him for child support? Or what if she even now were to file a report as to statutory rape—no matter how hard he'd lie about her deliberately seducing *him,* sixteen years of age was definitely below the statutory age of consent.

Barb knew he had been in jail—but didn't know why. "He lies about everything," she'd said. "He claims he was framed—but he also claims that he didn't rape me!"

"It *is* Barb." He said the words out loud, almost shocked by the certainty that this was the cause of his unrest. Surprised, he repeated them almost in a whisper.

Something is very, very wrong.

He went to the prep room phone and called Van's office.

At the school, security personnel were busily checking each closet and storage area. Jana and a secretary went together to enter each women's rest room, and a janitor did the same for the men's. Jana had warned, "Even if we don't see feet under a door, we've gotta check to see if it's locked. Barb said she could stand on the john, so her feet wouldn't show. I said that was a real dumb idea, for what would happen if her foot slipped, especially with her being pregnant and everything...."

Vanessa had to consciously keep herself from pacing as she waited with Nancy in the outer office. She'd already checked again with her mother's office, but got the same information. Seeing movement beyond the glass, she fleetingly thought it might be Jana or one of the others already returning—but then a ripple of relief went through her.

It was Rob coming in, heading right for her, holding out both hands. "I called your office because I was worried about Barb. Suz told me I'd find you here. Are you all right?''

Her hands slid into his, and held tight. ''Barb's missing. A red car came right at her this morning, and she's probably too scared to think straight!''

''Have you called the police?''

''Not yet—but I'm afraid we'll have to, even though I can't get hold of Mother. I wanted to wait until they've checked all possible hiding places here at the school.''

She gave him a brief rundown of what little they knew, and by then Jana had returned, followed almost immediately by the others. They'd found no trace of Barb.

''Y'know, if this were *me*,'' Jana volunteered, ''I'd have headed back to Gram's.''

''You *would?*'' That surprised Vanessa. ''But she'd be alone, out in the open, on Sylvan Falls's sidewalks for a number of blocks, fully exposed to *anybody* looking for her.''

Jana ducked her head as though embarrassed by having made a poor suggestion, but then her neck and shoulders straightened. ''There's just something that makes you want to be there if you're scared—it's like going *home* should be. I'd feel safe just because it's Gram's place, and *yours*.''

She couldn't help it; Vanessa, who had always felt too stiff and in control to be demonstrative, was hugging the girl. "That's one of the nicest things anyone ever said to me—that I might give you some feeling of security, of being home."

"But you *do*, Vanessa. Who else would have moved in to take care of the five of us, especially since you have all that really *important* work to do?"

She accepted the handkerchief Rob handed her, blotted the tears running down her cheeks, and cleared her throat. "Nancy, I'd like to take Jana home with me if that wouldn't be counted as an unexcused absence."

On learning it would be regarded as excused, she gave the other woman her business card, writing on it both Gram's and her mother's phone numbers. She'd have left then, but Nancy wanted them to call police headquarters from there, and she would get both the principal and the school district's lawyer to sit in on what was said.

"After all," she stated, "if the car in question came from our parking lot, we *are* involved, even though we had no part in it. It's even possible that the driver may prove to be a student here—in which case this might be a matter of teen lack of control, rather than a deliberate, malicious act of violence."

Vanessa started to say they were fairly sure who it was, but Rob suggested, "Perhaps some of those students who saw the incident can give information, too...."

Rob was the one who put through the call to the police chief, a fellow member of the local Lion's Club. "Hi, Lew, it's Rob here... No, nothing to do with me professionally, but we do appear to have a problem here at the high school. One of Gram McHenry's girls was nearly run down by someone in a red car... We're not sure, but there's a distinct possibility it could have been intentional... I'd rather wait till you get here... Right away? Great! We'll be in Nancy Foresman's office."

Vanessa reached for the phone right after he'd replaced it, asking Nancy if it was okay to call home—to call Gram's house. "I should have checked earlier, in case Barb did go there."

When Aunt Phyl stated that Barb had neither called nor come, Vanessa asked if she'd check with the other three girls. There was the slim chance that one of them could have seen her if she had come in the front door and gone right to her room. "Look, have them check everywhere. Barb was almost hit by a car this morning, and she's bound to be scared.

"Since she doesn't seem to be here at school, the most logical guess is that she'd go there. However, if she didn't want you to know she's skipping school, she *could* be hiding somewhere, even in the basement or attic.''

''That seems highly unlikely, dear.'' Aunt Phyl sounded as calmly reassuring as she undoubtedly was with difficult patients at the hospital.

''I know, but she came to school with Jana—yet never showed up at her home room. We're past the probable places to look for someone who's panicked, so we're considering *possible* ones—like even in the loft over the garage.''

''You're really serious about this, aren't you?''

''Dead serious!'' *And I used that awful word again!* ''Jana's here with me, and Rob. The police should be arriving any moment now, so if you find Barb, call me here at the school office right away.''

''And—if *you* do, let us know, too.''

Her aunt's voice had been low, troubled, but Vanessa had no reassurance to give.

Lewis Fredricks was the only police chief Vanessa could remember; she respected him, but didn't know him well as a person. ''How's your grandmother?'' was the way he greeted her, and Vanessa, convinced that he really wanted to know, briefly filled him in on how Gram was doing.

They trooped into the principal's office, the lawyer, Jason Somerville, entering right behind them. There was no longer a possibility of not sharing

Barb's long-term fears, as well as what had happened that morning.

Lew stated that he should have been notified earlier, and the school officials also said they'd have appreciated such a courtesy. It was all Vanessa could do to keep from squirming on her seat, but Jana was sitting on her left side and Rob to her right.

It was he who explained, "Everyone was in a bind, Lew. As Van told you, *nothing* had been done back home about this then sixteen-year-old's being raped again and again. Her mother did sign papers so Barb could come here." His shoulders lifted in a shrug as he suggested, "Perhaps just so she'd not have responsibility for whatever happened.

"Both her mother and that jerk threatened her with dire consequences should Barb tell anyone what took place—the man even threatened to kill her and her mother if she breathed one word about it! Is it any wonder she pleaded with us to just leave things as they were?

"Even *that* was just recently, when she thought he might have followed her here. But that hardly made sense to us. Why should he come now? As far as he could see, he was home free...."

There was much give and take. An announcement went out over the PA system telling anyone who saw the almost-accident this morning to report to the office at once. Only two boys showed up, together, each claiming that all he knew was that it was an unfamiliar red car with Pennsylvania plates, containing numbers he didn't remember. Neither boy got a good look at the driver's face, nor could he remember any distinguishing features, marks, or anything.

And then the call came from Aunt Phyllis; Barb *had* unlocked the front door, *had* come into the hall and up the stairs to her own room. Then, fearing that someone just might see her, however, she'd crept up the second flight of stairs, into the attic. AnnaMae found her there, sitting on the floor in a back corner, holding a broken-headed doll.

Barb looked pale and drawn when Vanessa first saw her after arriving at Gram's, but Barb insisted she felt all right. Vanessa tried to get a better picture of what she'd been going through, but Barb wasn't sharing *anything* about what had happened—nor her response to it. She clearly felt betrayed by Vanessa telling the school authorities and the police things she'd wanted kept secret.

She still had the doll from the attic with her, and Aunt Phyl asked Vanessa if this might have anything to do with Barb's thinking ahead toward her own infant's birth. "But I don't even know where that doll came from, do you? I can't remember ever even seeing it.''

Vanessa didn't want to talk about it, but Aunt Phyl had been so good…. ''It may have been mine, given to me when I was still quite small. I had one that got broken soon afterward.''

''Oh, that's too bad.'' But then her face brightened. ''There was a doll doctor who came to a women's meeting I went to not long ago. You might want to check with her about getting the doll repaired.''

Vanessa forced a laugh. ''Thanks, but I'm not going to bother. I never did play much with dolls, and didn't form an attachment with any of them. It had to be Gram's doing that it has been saved all these years.''

She ate a sandwich on the way back to her office, and was grateful when Suz made a fresh pot of coffee. Raising her mug in salute, she headed through the doorway for her own desk. ''Now if you can just keep me from any and all interruptions, your coffee and my determination will at least get the phone calls returned and maybe even some of those papers from my in-box, *out*.''

''Oh, *sure*—and if I'm that good at controlling time and circumstances, I'm going to stop on the way home and buy a ticket to the state lottery! I hear it's up to eight million bucks this week!''

Vanessa laughed, too, for neither of them gambled. She sat down and didn't move from her seat for the next two hours—and then it was to finish going around to the various departments. By the time she'd completed this and found things in good order, it was almost too late to go see Gram before heading home—yet she *had* to, even if only for a few minutes.

Her grandmother was lying in bed, looking exhausted from the therapy session she'd just come back from. She perked up at once, however, and reached out her arms as Vanessa entered the semiprivate room. "It's so good to see you, dear. I was just thinking of—and praying for you. How is everything?"

Where do I even begin after a day like this? Vanessa wondered. She leaned over to permit the hug and to kiss the cheek of this woman she loved so much. "First of all, thanks for the prayers—this was one day I'm not sure I'd have got through without them."

"Oh?" Gran fumbled for the bed control and tilted the top higher. "What happened?"

Vanessa had to force herself to remember how soon she must leave, but tried to tell the high—or *low*—points. She finished by saying, "I'm not sure I did what you would have, Gram, but under the circumstances I had to tell the authorities. And the school."

Gram's response was a slow nod of the head before saying, "You did fine, dear. I suppose we should have done that earlier, but sometimes sensitivity gets in the way of common sense." Her smile was of encouragement, not mirth. "I'm proud of the way you handled this."

"Rob and the school officials seemed to think this was the only thing to do—since we hadn't before. But when it came right down to doing it, I found myself pretty much alone."

"That's the way life is—we get little practice sessions, but then the time comes when we have to simply step out in faith and do what must be done. I suppose they'll have to interview Barb?"

Vanessa nodded. "*She* has to know that, too. That's probably why she hid up there in that stifling heat, too scared to face them alone."

"If only I could be with her—with all of them...."

Vanessa squeezed her hand. "We wish you were able to be there, but it's essential that you get therapy twice a day. We want you to have the most complete healing possible—to get back to where you were before."

"They've made no guarantees of that."

"They can't, I suppose, but we both know

they're *very* well pleased with your progress, and your gumption. They'll let you return as soon as possible.''

"I guess so.'' But then Gram gave a soft little laugh. ''Everyone complains about hospitals sending patients home too soon, but I promise you won't hear one word of complaint from *this* patient when that happens.''

Chapter Eight

Vanessa pulled into the alley and parked outside Gram's garage. She was tired, mentally and physically, and so emotionally exhausted that she longed to just go to bed and pull the covers up over her head.

Opening the car door, she got out and forced herself to walk more briskly than she wanted to. Inside the kitchen, the table was already set, for *nine*, she noticed, and there were boxes and a double-layered cake-and-pie carrier on the counter.

AnnaMae came hurrying into the kitchen. "I thought I heard you," she greeted, then turned to call into the hallway, "Hey, everyone, Vanessa's home!"

There were quick footsteps approaching as Vanessa laid her purse on the sideboard. "It's good to be back."

Kate, Jana and Ricki joined them, then Gin Redding, who'd again relieved Aunt Phyl—and, almost unbelievably, there was her *mother,* hand in hand with Barb!

Although feeling bug-eyed with surprise or shock, Vanessa made a concerted effort to keep things as normal as possible. She smiled at the last arrivals, but her, "I apologize for being a little later than usual, I stopped to see Gram on my way home," was for all of them. "As far as I can tell, she's doing better, and sends her love to each of you."

"Have they told her yet when she can come back?" Ricki asked.

"Not yet—but you know doctors. They hesitate to give an estimated time, then have to disappoint patients. One of these days he'll come in and say, 'This is the day. You can leave this morning.'"

"I sure hope that will be soon!"

That had been Barb's voice Vanessa heard, along with others. "I agree...the sooner the better!"

She caught the look on her mother's face, which had to be an expression of sympathy, or empathy, but Jana was piping up with, "I'll bet you do hope that, Vanessa! You must miss *awfully* being at your own apartment, free to come and go and do whatever you want."

She cleared her throat, needing that fragment of time to sort out what to say. Yes, that would be good, but... "When that time does come, I'm going to miss every one of you. You've become important, wonderful parts of my life in this short time."

She wanted to know how Barb was doing, but might have to wait until later for someone to fill her in—for just then the person who would probably be sitting at the unaccounted-for ninth table setting came through the hallway. Gin stated with satisfaction, "Ah, now that Rob's here, we can eat!" She looked back toward Vanessa. "He delivered this meal from Miz Aggie, too, and it smells so good we could hardly wait."

Apparently I've been missing out on a tremendous amount of fellowship in my life, Vanessa thought as boxes were opened, food placed on the table, prayer said, and the eating begun. Surprising herself again, she caught herself thanking God for second chances—or it could be the hundred-and-second chance for all she knew! Apparently she hadn't been paying attention if or when they'd been offered.

Although there was much conversation, it did not even touch upon Barb, the notorious red car, nor her hiding! Paying special attention to her mother, whose presence at this table in Gram's kitchen still seemed almost unbelievable after those earlier years of estrangement between her and Gram, Vanessa realized that Paula was especially alert, missing nothing. She didn't introduce subjects, but readily responded when addressed.

Rob stated during dessert that it must by now be his turn to clear away things tonight. Vanessa started to say that wasn't necessary, but stopped in time, realizing that four of the girls were already vying for the privilege of being his helper!

Barb joined the other three in the front room, sitting quietly on a footstool next to Paula, back to the windows. It took Vanessa only a moment to realize how deliberately this spot had been chosen, for no one on the street or sidewalk could know for sure that it was Barb sitting there.

Mother sat in a rocker, but Vanessa, with Gin talking to her, couldn't hear what the other two were saying. She'd brought the cordless phone with her, just in case she might need it—and of course it rang! At least she didn't have to worry that some emergency at the plant required her immediate presence, for she'd made arrangements with other capable personnel to be on call while she was here.

Gram was the one on the phone, and said she

was pleased that Mother had stayed for dinner and the evening. And, since Paula was still there, could she please speak with her?

Mother walked out into the hall, and their discussion seemed to be very serious and to go on for a long time. When she finally returned, it was to hand the phone to Barb. "She wants to talk with you, too."

It was obvious that Barb dreaded this, but she accepted the phone, managing a weak, "Hello, Gram," as she stood up. She, too, went to stand in the hall.

Vanessa asked, "How's Barb handling this, Mother?"

"Probably better than I could under the circumstances!" There was admiration in her voice, and even a slight smile on her face. "She still feels betrayed, even though she knows that what was said and done at the school was because of love— and let's face it, she's had little experience with selfless love!"

"Isn't this sad, Mother? It makes me wonder if she'll ever again be able to open herself to others."

Gin nodded. "I've fretted about that, too—but you know, she'd already changed a *lot* before Gram's fall. She's done a great deal of growing up—not counting today's mess."

Rob came in with the kitchen crew, all cheerfully trying to talk at once. For a moment Vanessa was almost sorry she'd not stayed in the kitchen with them, but everyone was together now, at least for a little while.

And instead of bringing in a chair, Rob was sitting cross-legged on the floor, beside her.

Having eaten late, the girls protested against being sent to bed at their accustomed time. Ricki tried to stretch it, saying, "Well, can we at *least* come back down here in our robes after we're washed up and changed? Couldn't we have our prayers down here, instead of upstairs?"

Gin beat Vanessa by saying, "That sounds like a good idea, doesn't it? It seems forever since my kids were still home and we used to have family prayers...."

Rob reached up to cover Vanessa's hand with his warm one. "I'd like that, too."

Her gaze turned toward her mother, apparently fascinated by a family picture on the piano. "All right—if you can all be back here in ten minutes."

Jana and Ricki almost bounded up the steps, Kate not far behind, while AnnaMae walked more sedately. Vanessa waited to ask her question until Barb, bringing up the rear, had turned at the landing to start up the second part of the long stairway. "Did you notice how Barb seemed to be almost *pulling* herself up each step, her hand on the rail and head tilted forward?''

Gin nodded. ''The poor child has had one dickens of a day! Hopefully things will be better tomorrow.''

''I was waiting to talk to you after they went to bed, Vanessa,'' Paula said, ''but I did spend one-on-one time with her before you returned. In addition to the scare she had, realizing she could very well have been killed this morning, she has no assurance at all that this won't happen again—and be successful.

''But what has her even *more* upset is her fear that you and Gram will give up on her after her hiding like she did and taking you from work much of the day—and with everyone being so worried.''

Vanessa, stunned, sat there staring at her. ''What in the world gave her that idea?''

Paula shrugged. ''She's a teen—and has already been rejected by the very people who should have cared for her. Since *they* couldn't be trusted, what basis does she have for believing that you or any of us can be?''

Vanessa sank back in her chair, feeling washed out, a failure. ''I thought—I'd hoped—we were getting through to her that we do really love her, that we want to help....''

Rob turned to look directly up at her. ''You're

doing a great job with that, Van. You *are*." He repeated it, apparently seeing her inability to accept that evaluation. "You've probably been more of a mother to that child than she's ever had in her life—and you're an advocate and friend. Please, Van, give her—and yourself—a break. It's impossible for her healing to take place in a couple of days—even months. You both need time. And rest."

"Rest! Oh, Rob, I can't even think straight right now. I'm *exhausted*...."

"Why wouldn't you be?" His voice was low, comforting in its reasonableness. "This mothering bit is such a new role for you, and requires so much but—" and he again gave that gentle, sweet smile "—you're doing a most extraordinary job! With Gram and you—and God—I truly believe Barb's going to be okay."

And Paula affirmed, "I, too, think she's going to make it. In my talking with Barbara—"

But Jana was already running back down the stairs, informing them, "Everyone will be here in a minute."

She'd plunked down on the end of the couch, nearest to Rob. Vanessa half expected Kate, coming next, to protest this taking of *her* seat, and was relieved when all the girl did was scowl.

She remembered to turn off the phone so prayer

time wouldn't be interrupted, but Rob's cell phone buzzed just as the last girls came down the stairs. He answered it from where he sat on the floor. After hanging up, he told them he'd have to be at the Laurel Heights Nursing Home within the next hour. Then he asked for another minute or two in which to call one of the retired men who helped as needed with funerals and other things. He was relieved to learn that Sam would be ready to go with him whenever Rob got there.

He turned off the electronic device and reached for the hands of both Vanessa and Jana. "I'm sorry about the interruption, but I would like to stay for prayers with all of you."

Vanessa nodded—and suddenly realized that she couldn't remember ever hearing her mother pray. Dad used to do that with her at meals and bedtime.

"Tonight we won't go right around the room as we often do, with each of us feeling *required* to pray. Let's just make it spontaneous—things we really want or need to say," she instructed. "Gin, would you please begin?" Then, looking down at the man whose hand was holding hers so firmly, and whose eyes were looking so warmly into hers, she added, "Since you've made arrangements to stay, would you please close our time together?"

They both nodded, and AnnaMae and Kate prayed after their neighbor. Vanessa felt dampness on her forehead and upper lip at the thought of doing this with Mother here, and Gin and Rob—but forced herself to do so. Surprisingly, once she began, she lost all sense of self-consciousness, of *performance*—it was just her and God together, and it was the most natural thing in the world to give Him praise, and to ask favors in the name of His son.

Rob left to change clothes, get the hearse, and pick up the body to be taken to the mortuary. Mother got to her feet, too, and surprised Vanessa by asking at the door, "Might it be possible for just the two of us to have lunch together soon?"

This was another first; there was no way she'd turn down this invitation. "I would like that."

It had been hard taking Barb to school the next morning, and she couldn't blame her for wanting to stay home. The girl said she didn't feel well, and Aunt Phyl would have been supportive, but Vanessa was afraid she'd have too much time to sit and worry. Hopefully they'd have a better handle on things after Mother's meeting with the police. She wished she could be there, too, but had not been included. "If you need to have Barb—and Jana, if necessary," Vanessa had suggested to her mother, "give me a call and I'll bring them."

Chapter Nine

Vanessa felt an urgency to get and keep her office work caught up, so found herself sticking to business-only on phone calls. She didn't like doing things this way, for she was convinced that her excellent relationship with wholesalers and individual customers was largely due to remembering not only her contacts' business preferences, but such personal things as a family member's illness or wedding.

She'd hardly begun clearing things away when she remembered that Andi and Keith had not been told of yesterday's happenings. She was reaching for the phone when there was the familiar tiny click of her intercom and she heard Suz's voice. "It's the school nurse, Van."

Now what? "Put her through, Suz...."

"Hi, Vanessa, it's Carol Parmenter, calling from the high school. Barbara Mutchler's lying down here in the office...."

"What happened?" She was on her feet. "Is she all right?"

"She's having a lot of abdominal pain. It apparently started right after she got to school, but she came here within the last five minutes."

"Is she hemorrhaging or anything?" *Please, God, not that!*

"Well, she is bleeding, but not much. However, her blood pressure's way over two hundred, and she's very frightened."

"Could the increased pressure be just from being scared? You may have heard about a car's almost hitting her yesterday."

"I'd heard some, and she's just been telling me about it." The nurse hesitated before suggesting, "I think she should be evaluated by a physician, Vanessa. She's not having regular contractions as of now, but says they *were* at fifteen and thirteen-minute intervals just before coming—"

"Can she ride in my car to the emergency room, or should I call for an ambulance?"

"She'd probably be okay in your car—but I'd opt for the ambulance if I were the one taking her."

"I'll call for that. Please tell Barb I'll be at the school as soon as possible."

Elmer had reminded Rob again this morning that washing the hearse had not been included as an item in their partnership contract, but Rob was out on the concrete parking area behind his house doing that. This was such a lovely, warm, sunny day that he welcomed an excuse to be out in it, wearing just shorts and beat-up sneakers.

He was officially off today, and considering what he would do next, since he'd nearly finished this job. It was then he heard the ring of the cell phone, which he'd placed on the driver's seat. Drying his hands on an old towel, he spoke into the electronic device. "Robert Corland here."

"Are you dreadfully busy right now, Rob?"

Vanessa! "No, I'm not. What's up?"

"I know I should be calling 911, but it's *Barb,* and I know how much she likes and trusts you, so I thought that *if* you had time, it might be best for you instead of someone else to take her by ambulance to the emergency room...."

Things are very wrong, Ron thought. Van never runs on like this! "What happened? That creep didn't find her, did he?"

"No, not that—but the school nurse just called. Barb's having abdominal pain, and she's bleeding, and her blood pressure's way too high. I said I'd call for the ambulance—and I'm heading over there right away.''

''Good. You go on, Van...Barb needs you with her. I'll call for someone to assist me and we'll be there as quickly as possible.''

''Thanks, Rob.'' He sensed her relief, especially when, just as she was leaving the phone, he heard her murmur, ''What would I ever do without you?''

In spite of the seriousness of Barb's condition, he experienced a surge of happiness. Van had just said, *What would I ever do without you?* which had to be among the most beautiful words he'd ever heard in his life!

Vanessa was tempted to stop along the No Parking stretch of curb so she could get to Barb as quickly as possible, but didn't know how long she'd be here.

She reluctantly drove clear to the far corner of the school parking lot before finding a vacant spot, and was running as she came back and went inside, grateful to find the nursing office where it used to be.

Carol led her into the small, pale-green area off the larger examining and treatment rooms, where Barb was lying on her back, eyes closed, but crying. Vanessa went to her, taking her hand. "I'm here, Barb...."

The girl's eyes opened, and she cried even harder, holding on to Vanessa's hand so tight it hurt. "Oh, Vanessa—I'm scared!"

"I know, dear. Things like this are always scary, but Mrs. Parmenter's a very good nurse, and she's taking care of you here. And Rob's coming in just a little bit." She thought Barb showed a little interest in that, so continued, "He's bringing the ambulance with him, so we can take you to the emergency room where someone can check you."

She'd tried to keep her voice quietly sympathetic, as well as reinforcing, but Barb's startled, "The ER? Is it that *serious?*" made Vanessa realize she'd proceeded too rapidly.

She pulled a chair over and sat down. "We have to make sure you're okay. You've been through a lot yesterday and today, which is probably why you're having these pains."

"Vanessa...?"

"What is it, dear?"

"My baby isn't—*coming* now, is she?"

There's pain in that question, not necessarily a physical one, probably something even stronger. "I don't think so, but that's why we need a doctor to check you."

"Can't you just take me in your car?"

Good question... "Ah, but Rob got to take Gram there, and now he's going to take you."

"I'm—scared of going in the ambulance. When *Gram* went, they kept her at the hospital, and she had surgery, and she's still there."

"But *you* don't have a broken hip, Barb, and you're not in your seventies, either."

That earned a weak smile. And then Rob was there, calling cheerfully, from the doorway, "Hey, Barb! What a nice smile with which to greet me!" He motioned over his shoulder toward the young man behind him. "Dick and I don't always get smiles when we come on the scene, so I'd say this is special."

He walked over and laid his hand on her tousled hair, asking, "How ya doing?"

"*Some* better, maybe." But then her face seemed to tighten and she sucked in her breath as her hand pressed against her abdomen.

Carol, on her other side, placed a hand beside the smaller one. "Is this pretty much like those you had in class, and the couple you had here?"

Barb nodded, jaw set. She didn't answer right away, and when she did she gasped, "*Each* one seems extrahard—" again she paused, holding her breath "—while it's here. I'm—not sure if it's worse."

"Well, how about our going for that ride now?" he asked.

She looked from him to Vanessa, who nodded slightly. "Are you coming, too?"

"Of *course* I am, but not in the ambulance. I'll be right behind you in my car."

Barb started to sit up, and her legs moved toward the edge of the bed, but Carol placed a firm hand on her shoulder, murmuring conspiratorially, "Let's let the men do what they're supposed to, okay?"

And Rob reinforced that with, "Yeah, we're *supposed* to take you lying down...otherwise, someone might think we're wasting time and gas by bringing the ambulance. You don't want us to get in trouble, do you?"

And the girl, apparently taking this at face value, agreed—although reluctantly.

While driving to the hospital, Vanessa called Suz first, then home. Gin assured her she'd stay as long as necessary, then added, "And give that poor little girl a special hug from me!"

Vanessa had never done much hugging, but there was no hesitancy in her agreeing to do that. She was almost to the ER parking lot when she called Andi, too. After all, it was the funding by

Andi and her father which had made Gram's work with the girls possible.

"I'm almost sure Barb will be admitted," she said, after giving a brief rundown of what had taken place. "I'll wait to stop by Gram's room until I know more, but I will have to fill her in then."

Andi sighed. "This will be hard on her."

"I'll do my best to be upbeat."

"I know you will, Vanessa. You've been great through all this, and I want you to know how much we appreciate it—and *you*."

"Thanks, Andi."

"We've been praying for you, dear, and will continue doing so."

"I'm going to count on that. There have been times of late when I'm not at all sure how well I'm doing, or how I'm going to get through the next tomorrow."

"But you *did* get through each of them, and now they're yesterdays...."

The ambulance was backed into one of the ER bays, and by the time Vanessa parked several rows away and got there, Barb was already being rolled through the automatically opening glass-and-steel doors, Rob and Dick joking with her about something.

Rob must have alerted the staff of their coming,

as an efficient young woman immediately led them into the second of three curtain-separated sections lining the left side of the very large area. Vanessa, however, had to go to the ER office in order to give all Barb's personal and financial data, which seemed to take an extraordinarily long time.

All three adults stayed while the physician was still examining Barb, until Rob's beeper sounded— and they learned that the ambulance was needed elsewhere. It was only a few minutes after Rob and Dick were gone that the decision was made for Barb to stay at least until tomorrow.

Vanessa went with her as she was rolled to a room on the surgical floor. Fortunately, the patient already there was a woman about Gram's age, and knew her through the literacy program. This seemed to make Barb less apprehensive, so Vanessa finally left, to go first to Gram's room, then head home to tell them there what was happening. *Somehow Gram's house does seem like home— more than my apartment or my parents' house or anywhere. Isn't that strange?*

She appreciated Andi's calling her there, to say she and her baby would spend the rest of the day at Gram's, so Aunt Phyl could have some time off. "I've been incredibly selfish, just reveling in being

Katherine's mother, and it's about time I start helping with some of the responsibilities!''

"Are you sure you're *ready* for this?"

Andi gave a little laugh. "My answer is that I want very much to be there. I'm not sure just what all's involved, but will do my best."

Vanessa's turning to tell the girls was met with a squeal of joy from Kate. "Oh, wow, *Katherine's* coming!" Great enthusiasm was expressed by AnnaMae and Ricki, as well.

"As you undoubtedly heard," Vanessa reported, "there's an air of expectancy hovering in our kitchen—and I'll remind them to help *you*, too—as well as to let you know what they might need help with as to their GED work."

They talked just a little more before Andi asked, "How do you think this emergency with Barb will affect Jana?"

She was glad she was using the cordless phone and could go look out the back door while speaking privately. "I drove them to school, of course, and know she's anxious—and she has every right to be. Even now, though we believe we know who was driving that car, in which case Barb's definitely the one he wants to silence permanently—we have no proof."

"Well, I'll do my best on the home front...."

"Just having the baby here will be a blessing, a wonderful distraction for the girls. Thanks!"

Vanessa was telling Suz of everyone's pitching in. "Can you *believe* these people?"

"Of course." Her secretary grinned at her. "I've known most of them for years and what they're doing sounds typical of them."

"Gram said pretty much the same when I talked with her for a few minutes after leaving Barb." She looked up from riffling through papers and notes on her desk. "Did I tell you they plan to teach her to get into and out of their car body tomorrow or the next day?"

"Their *car body?*"

"Mm-hmmm. The therapists have this body of an actual car—not the front portion, the *hood,* but most of the rest. Gram says that, from what she's seen, patients who are taught to manage that are soon discharged, so she's feeling real good about things."

"She's sure one spunky lady!"

"She always has been, and even more so now because she's determined to get back to her girls as soon as humanly possible." She'd found the paper she was looking for, and reached for the phone. "She also told me she was going down to the next floor to see Barb today. I don't know how she's gonna do it, but if I were a gambler I'd place odds on her achieving that...."

"Hi, Suz!"

She looked up as Rob crossed the outer office. "And a good morning to you, as well."

"Is the boss-lady in? Do you suppose I could bother her for a bit?"

"Only you, Robert Corland, know if you might *bother her,* but she's in there. If you want to chance it, be my guest." And she waved a languid hand toward the closed door.

Realizing she was making a special exception for him, he squeezed her shoulder as he passed. His knuckles rapped lightly against the heavy walnut door, which he was already opening as she was saying, "Come on in, Suz."

He poked his head around the door. "Can that invitation be for *me,* this time?"

She looked up, startled, but then her smile, that beautiful smile of hers, curved her lips and lighted her eyes. She stood up and started toward him. "Of course it can—it *is.*"

For a moment, as her arms came forward in welcome, he hoped she might walk into his, but was not surprised when she reached for his hands. Even this is more than I dared hope for, he thought. "I stopped at the hospital on the way back from getting information for a newspaper obituary. Gram's doing fine but—I'm not so sure about Barb.''

She took a step backward, eyes dark with worry. "Is she worse? Hemorrhaging?"

"No one called or anything?"

She shook her head. "*Should* they have?"

"I'm not sure. But if our ambulance monitor were to register what her infant's is, I'd be screaming for the best obstetrician I could get hold of!"

Her face paled, she let go of his hands and turned to get her purse from the bottom drawer of her desk. "I must go to her!"

"I did ask a nurse about it, and she went to check. I *hope* I'm wrong."

"But you don't think so."

"No." He followed her from her office and as they hurried though the outer one, she told Suz she was returning to the hospital. The phone rang and Suz answered it, then called after them, "Vanessa, wait! It's the hospital—they've got to talk with you!"

He walked back with her to Suz's desk, and held her unusually cold hand as she said, "This is Vanessa McHenry."

The person on the other end introduced herself, then stated that Barbara Mutchler was being taken for immediate surgery and, as Van was the one who'd signed her in, they needed her signature authorizing this.

"Authorizing *what?*"

"Well, whatever has to be done. She's hemorrhaging quite badly...."

"And the baby? What's happening with the baby?" she demanded.

"I—uh, don't know all the details, but we do need you here."

"Is the baby still alive?"

"I really can't tell you, though I do know that it's been going through a very stressed state."

"I'll be there."

She slammed down the phone, and Rob had to hurry to keep up with her as she ran out the door. "Let me drive," he suggested, but she shook her head and kept going. "Please, Vanessa, let me be with you."

He didn't want to tell her that in her present state it would be better for him to drive, but was relieved when she asked where he'd parked. "Right here in front of the building, in visitor's parking," he said, pointing. "It's as close as yours."

"But, then you'd have to stay...."

"I *want* to stay with you."

He had no way of guessing how she would interpret that, but she slid her hand through his arm and went with him. There was almost no conversation in the car. He tried unsuccessfully several times, and wondered if there was any chance at all that she might be praying, as he was.

At the hospital, they rushed up to Barb's floor, and found her bed empty. After speaking to the nurse who'd called, they learned that the baby—a girl—was dead. Also, Barb's blood pressure was almost off the charts, and the doctors had been unable to control the bleeding.

Rob tried to hide his dismay, his anger, his suspicion that perhaps there'd been carelessness in watching over the girl.

"Can I see Barb before she undergoes surgery?" Vanessa asked.

"I'm not sure," the nurse told her. "But I *do* know they need your signature."

Vanessa handed back the pen which had been put into her hand. "I'm signing nothing until I see her."

"But you must—really! They're getting blood for her, and they *should* have already begun surgery."

"Then take me—*us* to her. No one bothered to notify me until just a little while ago, and she's had far too much rejection in her life. I must let her know I care about her, that I love her!"

Rob's heart swelled with pride as they went together to surgery. Vanessa had to insist there, too, but did get to see the weeping girl before Barb was given anesthesia. He admired her even more now than before—and knew he loved her, that he wanted more than anything in the world to have her as his wife.

but she gave him too enduring a justification everytime she remembered the retirement party even now their feelings—and I knew he would see that this was my own fault pushing him to move to have at her work....

Chapter Ten

"They shouldn't have clocks in waiting rooms!"

"It probably wouldn't matter much, Van," Rob said. "How many people do you know who don't wear watches?"

"That's true." She sighed. "And when you come right down to it, perhaps it's good to actually see that second hand going around—each time it *does* represents another minute that need not be lived through again...."

He said nothing, and she was uncomfortable—perhaps he considered her overly negative. A change of topic was called for, so she said, "Right from the first, Gram wanted my name on all the documents related to starting and running this work with the girls. I didn't want to—in fact, *refused.* But you know Gram...she can be quite persuasive when she has her mind fixed on something!''

"I've noticed. I'd probably find it very annoying if we weren't usually on the same side."

She briefly returned his smile. "I must admit I usually am, too. But in this case I was sure she was wrong. She *had* to be, didn't she? I'm an only child, I know next to nothing about dealing with teens and haven't been around them since I was one myself, I've never been pregnant or been kicked out of my home or been rejected by a lover."

How did I let myself say that? That was a spasm of pain crossing his face; he undoubtedly remembers when I rejected his proposal! "I mean, how could I hope to relate to them? How could they trust or even like someone like me who, from their point of view, has everything?"

"So—" he looked puzzled "—what did motivate you to sign those papers?"

"*Love,* I guess—though I never asked myself that. I thought she'd go ahead and ask Aunt Phyl or Andi or Karlyn—*any* of them being more qualified."

"You're selling yourself short, Van. Again."

She found herself squirming, and pushed herself back against the couch, sitting up straighter. Why did you have to add that last word? she thought. You, too, must be remembering the night when we—I—decided to stop dating.

"But she didn't, even though that brought the process to a halt for a while. My mother had done so *much* for the cause—all on a volunteer basis, I'll have you know, even when Andi and her father wanted to pay her."

"Why did that surprise you? It's a very good cause."

"But she *hated* being a mother." She saw the expression on his face and rushed in more words. "I'm not saying she hated *me*, but she wanted none of the responsibility of caring for or raising me. That was Dad's job—and he did his best."

"Well, whoever it was did a masterful job."

She covered his hand lying on the couch next to her own. "I wasn't asking for sympathy, Rob, even though I suspect it sounded that way."

His hand turned under hers, fingers working their way between hers, clasping them warmly. "I didn't think you were—that would be out of character."

She went back to the beginning of this conversation. "I finally signed all those papers because I love Gram, probably more than any other person in the world. No matter what happened or with whom, whether I got good grades or not so good, if my world was rosy or cloud-filled, I always knew Gram loved me.''

He nodded, and she wondered if he really could understand how important this was. ''I didn't seriously consider anything really bad happening to her—that she'd be unable to function in her usual brisk, capable way. Certainly not for years and years, anyway—perhaps after she'd lost interest in keeping up *this,* another of her good works.

''And then the broken hip, and the responsibilities with the girls and then Barb's fears! How could anyone have expected that vicious paramour of her mother's attacking her *here?* And, now, her losing her baby girl!'' She drew in a deep breath, which ended with another sigh.

''She's had no chance to bond with the baby yet—or anything.''

''Not in the sense of holding the baby in her arms or singing lullabies, perhaps, but she has carried this little girl beneath her heart, in the warmth of her body for about six months. Knowing it's there, coming to a new community with all new people, going to school and creating a life for herself here, *all* for the sake of her little one.

''I'm afraid this is going to hit her very hard— she may have doubts about what her life's worth if she can't even bring forth her own little baby into the world.''

He slipped his arm around her shoulders and drew her to him. "Poor dear Vanessa, you're *shivering*."

Her forehead was against his shoulder. "I feel so bad for her—she now has a 'broken' baby of her own."

"What?"

She didn't pull away, just snuggled more closely against him as she told of Barb's finding the doll in the attic. "I wonder if she might..."

"Might what?"

"Oh, I don't know." But she continued, "Is it possible she sensed that something might be going wrong with her pregnancy? With her baby?"

"I doubt it. She had enough to worry about ever since seeing that red car."

She nodded. "And with Gram in the hospital."

"Even with Gram in the hospital, she still has you. And she has Gin and Phyl and all the rest of us. Actually, if this was going to happen, it's good it happened here.

"At least we'll hope and pray that Barb, herself, will be all right. And we'll be here to help in every way possible."

The big hand was well on its circling of the clock's face for the second time when Gram arrived in her wheelchair. "Who brought you?" Rob demanded.

"Never underestimate the power of a determined woman, young man." Her grandmother shook a finger at him, while trying not to smile. "I called the switchboard and asked what room Barb was in, then rolled myself to the elevator and went there.

"She has a most cooperative roommate, who informed me that Barb had been taken to surgery and that a handsome young couple had been looking for her and were coming up here. Therefore, I got myself back on the elevator and came."

"You feel proud of yourself, don't you?" Vanessa asked.

"You bet I do!" Gram beamed at them. "And I'm about to tell them in therapy that if I can do all this, there's no reason for them not to send me home almost immediately!"

Rob laughed. "A couple of us were saying yesterday that we must get around to building that ramp up to your back door—that would be simpler than to the front one, if that's okay with you?"

"Perfect!"

"We expected to have another week or more, but I guess we'd better get on the ball!"

"Ah, yes, that would be excellent. Maybe if I tell them that's all ready and waiting, they'll release me a day or two earlier.'' And then she added, ''Oh, there's something else, too. They're trying, not too successfully, to teach me to go up and down steps—but there's no *way* I'll negotiate my home's long flight in the foreseeable future.

''So what are the chances of getting your ramp builders to bring my bed and dresser down to the rear of the dining room?''

He pretended to give that consideration. ''I think our ramp builders can handle that.''

''Good!'' And with that taken care of, Gram brought the conversation to the reason for all of them being here.

No, they'd heard nothing so far. And when they realized no one on Gram's floor knew where she was, Vanessa went to a nurse to request that she call the others, reporting that their patient was here—and that she was staying until they found out *exactly* how Barb was doing!

It wasn't much later that they learned Barb was in the recovery room doing ''as well as could be expected.''

''So you found me, George,'' Gram greeted the man coming in the door.

''Yes, but it's *you* who's supposed to be getting exercise, not me!'' The complaining tone the young man from therapy was trying for was belied by his grin. "And here I am with a wheelchair from my department and you already have yours...."

"No problem at all, you go ahead and push yours—or *ride* in it if you like—while I get a head start on my exercises by supplying my own power."

He laughed, as did Vanessa and Rob, who walked along with them to the elevator, promising to let Gram know when Barb was returned to her room. On their way back, Rob tried to hand Vanessa his keys. "I'll have to leave as soon as we see Barb, so you take these."

She came to a full stop and stood there, hands behind her back, staring up at him. "And how, pray tell, are you planning to return? *Walk* all that way?"

She looked so stubborn that he reached to cup her cheek with his palm. "Elmer or someone will come for me."

Her lower lip was thrust out just a little as it used to do way back then, and he had the almost uncontrollable desire to lean over and kiss her as she stated, "I, too, must get back to work as soon as Barb's awake enough to know that we stayed through surgery, that we were *here* for her."

She'd called Suz twice, and was able to answer some questions and give messages, so things weren't stacked up too badly by the time she got to the office. For that matter, she even got home only a little later than usual.

She'd kept Andi informed as much as possible, but the girls demanded a recap of her day, which she tried, unsuccessfully, to keep brief. They were deeply concerned for Barb, and cried over her baby's death.

Vanessa couldn't help wondering if all their grief was for Barb—or could it be partly for themselves, as well? And was the loss of *her* infant made even more poignant because of Andi's baby, the very much alive, beautiful, cuddly little Katherine, right here in this house with them, being passed from one to another with such tenderness and love?

The more she thought of this, the more she fretted, and determined to discuss this concern with Gram the following day—and probably with Mother, too. Would any of the girls back out on her commitment to give up her baby? If so, what would be the future of that mother and her child?

And to the future of this undertaking of Gram's...?

Morning—but it didn't feel like it! Vanessa looked at the clock-radio and stifled a groan. That early-morning light of those good long days of summer and early autumn was over until daylight saving time ended in another few days.

I'm not ready to get up, but if I go back to sleep and am awakened by the alarm in less than an hour, that will be even worse, Vanessa thought.

But she did—and it was! This time, however, there was no time for anything but to be up and ready for the day. She was grateful for Gram's insistence from the beginning that each girl take responsibility for her own waking and getting around, so things progressed normally.

AnnaMae wanted to call the hospital, but Vanessa reminded her that Aunt Phyl would soon be here. Having been on duty last evening, she could tell them how Gram and Barb were then, and could even get a morning update, should she desire to do so. Vanessa did, though, request that someone call her at work with whatever additional information they might get.

Jana was unusually quiet while being driven to school, but only when they were nearly there did she admit how much she missed Barb. "Sometimes we almost hate each other and sometimes we fight, but I like her a lot, Vanessa—I really do!"

"I know." She smiled at the teen beside her and reminded, "You may have to tell her teachers why she's not there."

"They must know already—the ambulance came and took her to the hospital right from the school!"

"That's true, and I did notify the school office this morning, but it's okay to tell them in case they missed it somehow. And even if they're aware of *that,* they probably haven't heard about her surgery, and her baby's dying."

Jana's eyes, already red, started to fill with tears again. "If they ask questions or—or anything, I'll probably start bawling again...."

Vanessa wanted to give encouragement but said honestly, "I wouldn't be surprised if that happens to all of us."

"I don't want to be a crybaby." It was almost a wail.

"None of us wants that, including me." She leaned over to squeeze Jana's hand. "I used to consider tears a sign of weakness, or of asking for sympathy, and tried to never show how much I was hurting. I'm only just now, as old as I am, learning that it's okay to grieve. I trust it won't take you this long."

There was a brief pause as Jana's mind apparently allowed this room in her consciousness. "What did you used to grieve about?"

"A number of things, actually. The accidental death of a dear friend when I was very young. The fact that my parents weren't happy together, and I always felt in the middle of that—maybe even the cause of it somehow. Grandad's dying in a fire while trying to rescue a friend. A romance which— was broken...." *What am I doing, sharing with this child my secret sorrows?*

She was glad to be pulling to a stop there at the school before she made an even greater fool of herself, but it was then she heard the very small voice from beside her. "I'm sorry, Vanessa. We had no idea *you* had such sadness in your life, too. No wonder you're such a cool person. You understand—that's why we love you so much!" That said, Jana got out of the car and hurried up the walk.

Thank goodness Jana's not looking back! It's bad enough if others see tears running down my cheeks, Vanessa thought as she grabbed several tissues from the box beside her, scrubbed the wetness away and blotted her eyes. It wasn't remembered pain that had brought them, but the words, the *sympathy* of this young woman who daily lived with the consequences of her own mistakes, and the rejection of her family.

Oh, God, help her, she pleaded, hardly recognizing this as prayer. *Help all of us*—please! *I don't know how to deal with any of this....*

* * *

"It's not fancy, but this place is great for lunch. It has good food and quick service," Paula said, leading the way to a back booth in Betty's Tea Room. "Have you been here before?"

You don't remember.... "Well, you did bring me a few times when I was little. They used to have tiny, warm, delicious cinnamon rolls, and a woman came around with long silver tongs, replacing each one I ate."

"Ah, yes. Betty's sticky buns have kept countless numbers of us loyal through the decades!"

"Is she still around? Still doing that?"

"Look and see." There was a smile on her lips and a sparkle in her eyes as she nodded toward a small, smiling woman, at least in her mideighties, carrying a silver tray from which she was transferring to each patron's side dish the delicacies about which they'd been speaking.

It wasn't until they'd received theirs and placed their orders that they even spoke about Barb's situation, and Paula told her daughter it was good that she was continuing to drive Jana to school, since she was obviously upset and worried.

And they talked of Gram and Gin and the other girls—and of Rob. "I take it he's more than just a friend?"

"I'm not sure—and I'm not trying to be evasive," Vanessa added quickly. "I do like and respect him, and he's been around a lot, but that's mostly because of his being involved from the very first when Gram fell. He was the EMT in charge."

She took another bite of her sticky bun. "And he's been wonderful about delivering meals and just being—around." I sound as immature and repetitious as an early teen with a first boyfriend! she thought. Seeing the look in her mother's eyes and the slight smile, she knew Mother had her own interpretation of their friendship. And of course she'd be remembering that they'd dated in the past.

But they talked no more about this, either, keeping the conversation casual as they mentioned things connected with family and friends. The important part, she decided once she was again back in her office, was that they could now at least talk about *something*. Even though they were still far from being close, there'd been nothing unfriendly about their hour together.

She'd run out of time to phone home before rushing off to meet her mother for lunch but, as she was reaching for the phone to do that, Vanessa received an incoming call. Jana was at the police station; she'd just been caught shoplifting!

Chapter Eleven

I can't handle all of this! It's too much....

She'd never considered the possibility of one of the girls leaving school without permission, much less shoplifting! How had this happened, anyway?

She didn't mention to Suz where she was going or why, just that she'd be back. Although Vanessa felt sure from her raised brows and amused smile that Suz had jumped to an erroneous supposition, she did nothing to correct it. She had left a message on her mother's voice mail, so Mother would certainly contact her directly or come to the police station instead of calling here.

As she drove across town and parked in the large macadamized parking lot, she tried to figure out what had gone wrong. It had been distressing when

Barb got into the house with no one knowing it—and now Jana had secretly left school and got in trouble! Vanessa had been living in a fool's paradise as to her ability to keep her charges safe and secure—*and* as to their willingness to obey rules.

She went up the shallowly slanted ramp to the door of the police station and opened it, then walked purposefully to where a short, plump woman of about her own age was sitting behind a large, organized-looking wooden desk. "I'm Vanessa McHenry. I believe you were expecting me."

The woman pushed herself to her feet. "Thank you for coming. Just follow me," she instructed, and led the way down a corridor to the second door, which was wide-open. "Chief Fredricks, this is Vanessa McHenry."

He'd been sitting at the side of the table. Jana, looking terribly frightened, sat at its end. He stood up, but leaned over to lay his hand on Jana's shoulder and shook his head when she, too, started to rise.

He nodded toward Jana. "We seem to have a problem here."

"That's what I was told." How does one handle a situation like this? she wondered. "Am I allowed to speak with her?"

"Of course."

"I tried reaching our legal counsel on my way here, but had to leave the message on her voice mail. May I please try again?"

"You may."

The fact that he didn't leave the room turned out not to matter, since Mother was still not answering. "What did Jana do?"

"She was observed stuffing something into her backpack and paid for only two other things at the checkout. The assistant manager of Nesbitt's General stopped her out on the sidewalk and politely asked Jana to show him what was in her bag—and she refused. So we were called, and I brought her here."

She sat there looking at Jana, who continued to stare down at the tabletop, two tears at a time tracking down her smoothly rounded cheeks and making darker blue spots on her loose-fitting top. Vanessa pressed the redial button on her phone and hoped desperately for her mother's response— which didn't come.

I don't know what to do! she thought. And then she almost heard Gram's voice saying words that she'd ignored at the time: "There's too much going on that I don't understand. I'd go crazy if I didn't know I could go to God and ask for help— and know He *wants* me to ask."

Okay, God, it's me, Vanessa, the one who was

always too proud to even ask for things, much less praise or honor You. If You don't help me now, I'm afraid I'm going to really mess things up— make matters even worse. Please, Lord, give me wisdom.

There had been no response from Jana, not even a visual one other than the tears, so Vanessa drew in a deep breath and asked, "Did you steal from the store, Jana?"

The girl's chin was almost to her chest, and she didn't look up as she whispered, "Yes."

"What did you take—and *why?*"

"I didn't *intend* to steal anything. I honestly didn't plan to do that when I left school."

She looked slowly upward until her tear-reddened eyes met Vanessa's with such misery that the woman longed to reach out to her—but had to ask, "Then why *did* you leave?"

She squirmed on her seat. "I—was lying in bed this morning, thinking of the baby. Barb didn't have anything for her, not a receiving blanket or an item of clothing—not *anything.* So when I was getting ready for school I thought I'd take all the money I had—which wasn't very much!—and maybe I could go to Nesbitt's after school."

Jana looked at her hands again, but then her glance flicked upward to meet Vanessa's for just a moment. "But while I was in study hall I wasn't able to study at *all*. I couldn't get out of my mind that Barb's dear little baby girl had nothing to wear when she's buried. And I got to thinking that maybe I should go to the store during the day, for Aunt Phyl would worry a whole lot and probably call you and Gram if I didn't get home when I'm supposed to.''

She was wringing her hands, and Vanessa didn't bother to ask permission before reaching out to hold one of them. "Go on, Jana. You left school and...?"

"And I was *real* scared that people would recognize me and ask why I wasn't in school. But I had to do it *today*, of course, so I could tell Barb this was taken care of.''

Of course? Couldn't you have asked us? Why wouldn't you know that anything like this would most certainly be taken care of? Vanessa silently wondered. She made an effort to keep her facial expression and voice free of censure as she nodded and asked, "So—what did you do then?"

"I went into the store and back to the baby things—and they do have some cute stuff there, Vanessa. I looked through all of it—but most were too big for a tiny preemie!

"And then I found one just right, and *white*, like I wanted, 'cause she's such a pure little innocent baby. It has narrow shoulders, and a nice long skirt that would come down and cover her feet, so she wouldn't need booties or anything.

"At first I thought of asking if you'd loan me money, 'cause it cost *way* more than I had."

"I wish you had called," Vanessa murmured.

Jana's, "Me, too!" was emphatic. "There was also a pretty little lace hat for her, something like the one Aunt Phyl found for Barb to put on the doll she found in the attic—to cover the broken part of the doll's head, you know. And there was a nice little rattle."

Vanessa's unshed tears were nearly choking her. She could only nod encouragement.

"But everything was so expensive! The lacy hat and the rattle took almost all my money—and I was scared someone might come and buy that little white baby dress, and it was the only one they had!"

Vanessa cleared her throat. "They probably would have saved it for you, had you asked them. And yes, I would have paid for it."

Jana seemed to suddenly remember the officer, who'd been quietly sitting off to the side. "Will you—have to put me in jail?"

His brown eyes met hers, then Vanessa's, then went back to hers. "Would you please show us, Jana, what you have in your backpack?"

She reached down to the side of her chair,

slowly lifted the canvas bag to her lap and released its straps. Vanessa could sense how painfully difficult it was for the child-woman to pull the flap upward, then lean across to give the opened backpack to the man.

Jana seemed to shrink down there on her seat, as the officer carefully, item by item, placed the contents on the table. "How much of this is...new...as of today?"

Vanessa appreciated his not using a term pertaining to stealing, and was relieved when Jana reached across, picked up the store's plastic bag, and removed a delicate little lace hat and an angel-decorated rattle, saying, "These are what I bought. See?" She held up the sales slip. "These I *did* pay for, and got back a dollar and four cents.

"But *this*," she continued, lifting out something neatly folded, white and of almost diaphanous texture, "I didn't have money to pay for—and I took it...."

Up until now, she'd kept her composure fairly well, but the emotional dam broke and she began to sob. Vanessa didn't ask permission, just went to her, holding her close. She had no words suitable for such an occasion, just crooned, "Oh, Jana, I'm so very sorry...."

She couldn't have told what or whom she was most sorry for—Jana, Barb, Barb's baby, the work she'd been trying to help Gram with, even herself.... She looked at the officer, who looked no happier than the others in this small room, but was saying nothing. She asked, "May I take her home with me?"

Jana turned to look at him, also, and he asked, "Jana, do you realize that what you did is wrong—that it was actually stealing from the people who own that store?"

She nodded, and tried to control her crying, as he said, looking her full in the face, "It's hard to know what's best, Jana. You do realize that what you did was wrong, and I should probably be taking you to the district justice."

Jana sank yet lower on her chair. Her eyes were huge, but she said nothing as he continued, "On the other hand, I can sort of understand what got you into this mess. The problem is that I'm not sure you've learned from the experience."

She sat up straighter, hope in her eyes for the first time since Vanessa had entered this office. "Oh, I *have*, I really have. I promise that I will never, ever, take anything from anyone else, even if I want or think I need it!"

"But what about—*this?*" The delicate lace gown seemed even more fragile with his big, strong hands holding it up by the shoulders. "What do you think should be done about this, Jana?"

"The—her baby deserves more than something stolen." She buried her face against Vanessa's shoulder as she cried, and the adults patiently waited for her to regain control. She was unable to look at either of them as she finally managed to reply, "I'll take it back to the store, confess and tell them I'll *never,* do such a bad thing again."

"Can you say that to them, Jana? And truly mean it?"

"Yes." She nodded, then looked up at Vanessa. "Would you go with me?"

There was so much pain in Jana's eyes that Vanessa had to agree. "Of course, but *you're* the one who will do all the talking."

"I know." Jana sighed again. "But your being with me would give me the strength to do it."

Rob was standing there looking out the window of the police station, praying, when he heard the sound of footsteps in the little hallway. Turning, he saw Vanessa first, then Jana and finally, Lew Fredricks. Vanessa's face seemed to light up as she saw him but he couldn't be sure for suddenly Jana was running toward him, wrapping her arms around him and buried her face against his chest. "Oh, Rob, I did something awful. I stole a little baby dress."

He looked over her head at the wonderful

woman who was saying in a voice almost too soft
to hear, "It's so good to see you!"

His heart swelled at the sincerity in her voice
and on her face. "I happened to be driving by, saw
your car outside, and thought perhaps I could
help."

Lew nodded a greeting. "We had a bit of a problem, Rob, but I think it's in the process of being
taken care of. Jana has been given the responsibility of making it right."

He wasn't about to ask questions, not now, not
here. "Are you ladies leaving?"

The girl looked at the officer with what appeared
to be pleading, perhaps hope? "*May* I go?
Please?"

"If I permit that, where would you go first of
all?"

"To Nesbitt's. For *sure,* to Nesbitt's first."

She is saying those words with certainty, yet her
look toward Van is questioning, Rob thought.

Vanessa nodded. "To Nesbitt's first, then back
to Gram's house."

Lew walked over and took Jana's hand, holding
it as he reminded, "I am trusting you, Jana, to not
only go to that store, but also to keep your other
promises. I'm counting on you to not get *me* in
trouble for letting you go."

"Oh, Chief Fredricks, I *will* keep my promises. And I'll never forget this day as long as I live."

He released her hand, but laid his on her shoulder as he looked into her eyes. "I trust you. You've got a lot going for you, my young friend, especially the people who love you. Don't blow it."

"I'm going to do my very best. I promise."

"That's what I like to hear." A genuine, warm smile was directed at her. "I hope to see and hear great things of you, Jana. Now go with God...."

I wonder how many other young people Lew's been instrumental in setting straight, Rob asked himself silently. Remembering Van's words, he felt free to ask as they were almost to her car, "Would you like me to come with you?"

Jana's eyes lit up, but Van shook her head. "No, but thanks, Rob, for offering. I'll be with her, but this is Jana's responsibility, and hers alone."

"All right—but I'll be praying for both of you."

"*That* we'll be grateful for, won't we, Jana?"

She drew in a big, fortifying breath. "Yeah. That and the cop's saying, 'Go with God.' I sure didn't expect *him* to say that."

Vanessa admitted she hadn't expected that, either, and Rob explained, "It's a different way of saying, goodbye. It's what *goodbye* really means, for that matter. Lew's a Christian, too, and I believe he'll be praying for you."

Jana nodded in agreement as she sank into the front seat of the car. After Jana closed the door Vanessa turned to Rob. "I dread going to the hospital to tell Gram all this, but I *can't* do it over the phone."

"Could you use some moral support? I'd be glad to go with you—as long as I can be back by six. The viewing for Steve LaCross is this evening."

She paused before saying, "That's not necessary, Rob, but I appreciate the offer. It's not your responsibility to hold my hand and give me courage."

"But I *like* holding your hand." He had to consciously refrain from adding that he very much liked holding *her*. "If it would help even a little, I'd like to go with you."

"Oh, it would *help*, all right, but I'm supposed to be a big girl now, and—"

"What time shall I pick you up?"

She gave a little laugh. "You tempt me, Robert Corland."

He'd like to respond differently, but asked, "What about four or four-thirty? It won't give us much time, but at least a few minutes."

"I've been out of the office too much already today—and oh, being so involved with this made me forget about Drew Barker, Andi's father, coming during late afternoon.''

"Well, what about this evening? If Gin can't stay on, perhaps we could find one of the church ladies to stay with the girls.''

"Oh, Rob!'' It was almost a wail. "I didn't even get around to asking Gin to stay till I got home! I got the call about Jana when starting to phone her about my probably being late.''

"It's okay, Van, you can do it now—and also check whether she can stay a little later *yet,* so you can go talk to Gram. If she can't do it, I'm sure we can find someone else.''

"I have no idea when we'll even be finished.''

"Well, call the funeral home when you're ready. Once everything's going smoothly with the viewing, Elmer can handle things.''

"I *shouldn't,* but I'm going to say yes. That way I'm sure to not let anything less than a major emergency keep me.'' She chuckled suddenly, unexpectedly. "And Drew will be even more interested in the expeditious handling of things than I am— he can hardly wait to see his adorable little granddaughter, Katherine!''

"It's a date!'' She did not respond to that, which of course she didn't need to. He suspected he'd shocked her by referring to this as a date; for that matter, he'd been a little surprised at hearing himself say it….

Chapter Twelve

Vanessa met Rob in the plant parking lot and they drove to the hospital together.

She was to be especially grateful for the comparatively lighthearted moments she spent with Rob, for the time they had with Gram was much more serious.

Gram sighed. "If only I were home...."

"How often I've wished that!" Vanessa confessed. "With being away so much, and spending many hours of my at-home time with helping them with studies, I can't seem to keep on top of things there. Had I paid more attention, perhaps I'd have realized things weren't right with Jana. I *did* notice her tenseness, but foolishly thought that was due to her almost being hit by that car!"

"I probably would have thought that, too."

Gram must be trying to make her feel less responsible for what happened today. "But you know the girls better than I do. You would have figured things out."

"Don't be too sure of that. Remember back to when you were a teen.... Do you think your parents had any idea of what was going on in your mind most of the time?"

"No, not at *all*—but our situations are entirely different."

"Not entirely. You, too, were a teen, much too proud and much too hurt to let anyone know the real you."

She stared at her grandmother. "You *knew* that? Back then you knew?"

Gram nodded. "Your grandfather and I hoped to love you into trust and confidence—and love—but you weren't ready."

She again felt that traitorous burning in her eyes. "And then Grandad died."

"And then Grandad died." She reached for Vanessa's hand as she repeated those words. "And for a time I was unfit, unable to help anyone."

"You missed him very much."

She nodded. "At the time, it seemed that no one could love him as much as I did—that nobody could be hurting as much as I." She squeezed her granddaughter's hand. "Forgive me for not understanding, for not trying harder."

"I loved being with you. You and Grandad, with your obvious love and *warmth* were the stabilizing center of my universe. I always half expected my parents' marriage to dissolve, but you and Grandad—" she could feel the little smile coming to her lips, and it was her turn to squeeze her grandmother's hand "—were *one,* like a single hyphenated word, *Gram-and-Grandad.*"

"I felt that way, too." Gram paused. "But then the hyphens broke...."

"Yes." Her voice was barely audible. "My hyphens broke then, too."

Rob had stayed in the background, and had to force himself to remain there now, to not draw closer, to enfold Van in his arms. He'd never suspected that *this* was the reason, at least *a* reason why it was after he'd proposed to her that she'd pulled away. Van had been afraid of being that close, that vulnerable; she was afraid of marriage!

He'd not read or heard of a "broken-hyphen syndrome"—but experts undoubtedly had some fancy name for that. He tried to remember, but couldn't recall hearing her speak of "Mother-and-Dad" together like that....

Van had said she must soon get back to the girls,

but they needed to stop first to see Barb. When
they arrived at her room, Barb was lying on her
back, eyes closed. As they approached her bed he
thought she was asleep, but Van whispered, "How
are you feeling tonight?"

Her hazel eyes were shadowed, haunted, but she
managed a weak smile as Van hugged her. "Better, I think—when I lie still." But then her face
contorted with pain as she bent her right knee by
sliding her foot upward on her bed.

"Then don't move much," Van suggested.

"They said I should—at least some."

"Oh." She gave a self-deprecating smile. "So
what do *I* know?"

There was the barest flicker of a responsive
smile. "I'm *trying* to do what they say. I want to
get home!"

"You're like Gram. We just left her, and she's
champing at the bit...."

"What's *that*?" Barb looked frightened. "Is she
all right?"

"I see I've already arrived at the old-timer stage
of life, Barb." Vanessa grinned at her. "That was
one of Grandad's expressions used to describe im-
patience with any restraints or delays—it's what
horses do when they're eager to get back to their
food or their stables."

The tiniest of smiles appeared on Barb's pale

face. "Yes, I'm—champing at the bit, too. Do you have any idea how long I'm going to have to stay here?"

"No, dear, not yet, but I doubt it will be very long."

"I hope not." She'd hardly paid attention to Rob until now. "Do you—have my baby?"

Rob was caught off guard. *I should have expected that, but...* "Yes, Barb, we do."

"Does she look okay? Is there anything *wrong* with her?"

He felt himself start to sweat and longed for some pat answer. "She looks fine."

"Then *why...?*" Tears were forming, almost instantly rolling down her temples to moisten her light hair.

He pulled several tissues from the box beside her, and reached to blot away some of the tears. "I don't have an answer to that, Barb. I wish I did." Oh, how I wish that! he thought. If she lost the baby because of being attacked by that car—if her mother's lover was the cause of it, I'd do almost anything to make sure he pays!

Perhaps Barb was thinking along those lines, too, for she was asking, "Does she have bruises or broken bones—or *anything?*"

He shook his head. "None that I could see."

"Maybe when I was crawling through that

hedge to get away from the car—maybe my being so scared—or maybe I did something else that made her die...."

"Oh, no!" Van was holding Barb in her arms. "You did everything right—you did your very best to save her, as well as yourself. *Please,* dear, don't blame yourself."

Van was crying, too, and all Rob could do was put his arms around both of them, assuring each that she'd done and was doing the best she could.

Van apologized, sort of, in her own way, as Rob was driving back to the plant for her car. "I'm becoming a basket case, Rob—worn out from all this nervous tension and crying."

"You are definitely not a basket case, dear." He slowed down and came to a stop on the road's shoulder. Reaching across to unfasten her seat belt, he invited, "Come over here to the center."

He was almost surprised when she did as he suggested, without any comment, let alone objection, and he helped fasten the center belt. She rested her head on his shoulder, and his arm came around her. "I am so tired, Rob. I feel as though I could go to sleep and not wake up until the day after tomorrow."

"Will it be possible to do that as soon as you get home—go right to bed?"

"There's no chance of that. This and yesterday have been such *big* ones for all of us—filled with so many unexpected things. The girls will need to talk out at least some of them with me."

She sat up a little straighter on the seat, probably matching this to her thoughts. "I'm the only mother figure they have with them right now."

"With all due respect, my dear Vanessa," he said, starting to drive again, "you are not that much older than they."

"But from their point of view I have it *made*— an excellent position, a beautiful apartment—and it's good none of them has seen *that,* for they'd be impressed by all the wrong things—how much I must have spent on the high-quality furniture and *stuff,* rather than on how contented or happy I've been there."

He let the silence build for a bit, but they were coming up along the side of the plant, almost to where her car was parked. I don't have any right to ask, he thought, but... "So you haven't—been especially happy there?"

"Not nearly as much as I expected to be."

This time she did sit up straight, and he was almost forced to return his arm to its former position, with his hand on the wheel. There were so many obvious questions to ask or comments to make, but he was grateful when she stated, "It turns out that position and *things* aren't necessarily the most important factors in happiness. And fulfillment.''

''Then what *is?*''

He'd pulled into the spot just to the left of her car, and she was unbuckling her seat belt. ''Even as exhausted as I am, physically and emotionally, it is fulfilling to be needed, to be at least *trying* to help others.''

She looked at him for a long moment then, seeing him reach for his door handle, Vanessa requested that he remain where he was. She turned to open her door, and kept her hand on it even after she got out, murmuring, ''It is good to love—and to be loved.''

She closed the door very softly.

Chapter Thirteen

Vanessa permitted Jana to stay up longer than usual, so all four of her charges went to bed at the same time. She'd neglected to check with Mother and Gram about funeral plans or, for that matter, if there *was* to be a funeral and not just a burial. But that would have to wait.

She spread papers from the office out on the kitchen table, but gave up on them after finding herself going over several fairly simple ones several times before making sense of them.

She could still see Jana walking into that store today to confess to the owners what she'd done, and why. Vanessa was proud of Jana for offering to come in Saturdays or after school to do cleaning, or anything else they'd suggest, as a way to make up for having stolen the little dress she was now returning. They said they'd think it over and get back to Jana later.

Afterwards Vanessa's mother called to say that two of the boys who'd been behind Barb and Jana at the time of the attack, one being the person who'd thrown that rock, had gone to the police with the description of the car and driver. Along with the first two numbers of the license plate, their description matched that of Barb's mother's live-in boyfriend!

Vanessa was beginning to think a good night's sleep would help her as much as the girls—but then a soft knock on the front door startled her. Her heart raced for a moment before she saw by the porch light that it was Rob. She struggled to control her feet, not letting them run to the door, but she couldn't have kept from smiling had she tried.

They went into the front room together and sat on the couch, but Rob seemed somewhat strained, not as comfortable with her as usual. She finally asked, "What's wrong?"

"I must be more transparent than I'd hoped." He attempted a smile. "Were you aware of Barb and Gram wanting us to have a funeral for the baby?"

"I didn't know that, but it's probably a good thing."

His head cocked as he gave her his full attention, then slowly released his breath. "I was afraid you would be upset."

She almost asked why he'd think that, but caught herself in time. "I used to be quite outspoken about funerals, wasn't I?"

"You—*don't* mind?" There was still an element of surprise on his face, but he sagged back against the couch, obviously relieved. "I told Gram and your mother what you used to insist about funerals—that they were vestiges of past eras when people put on acts of weeping and wailing to impress others of how much they were grieving, and that this didn't give people the chance to even begin to get over the loss—all that sort of thing."

"Guilty as charged." She faced him directly. "But I now know that Barb needs this. From what AnnaMae says, she was hoping to somehow keep her little one, but now her baby's dead. She won't be able to nurse her or bathe her or anything—and she does need a funeral for her baby."

"That was Gram's opinion, too, after talking with Barb, who was crying for a number of reasons, including the fact that she has no money and couldn't pay for a casket, let alone anything else."

"And there's Jana, who even stole that dress for the infant to wear...."

"I took the liberty of taking care of the casket problem."

"You— How can you *do* that?"

"Several years ago, before I came back here to work with Elmer, the small child of a family originally from this area died while they were in Oregon. The infant was embalmed out there, and flown here in a small casket.

"However, the grandparents wanted something much more elaborate, and said Elmer should keep the first one until there was a case of real need."

"Actually, Rob, I'll gladly pay for it."

"I believe you *would* and so would Gram, or Andi, or the Deacons' Fund at the church. For that matter, I could myself. But isn't this better for Barb? This way she's not beholden to anyone, just using a nice little coffin that isn't doing anyone any good."

Her head cocked to the side as she considered his words. "You're probably right. You have so much more experience with grief—with those who are grieving."

There was silence for a moment, until she asked, "Will it be an open or closed casket for the actual funeral?"

"Probably closed for the funeral itself. But Barb does want to see little Vanessa."

The shock; the unbelief! "What did you say?"

His arm came around her. "You didn't *know?*"

She felt spaced-out, totally out of touch with reality. "She named her after *me?*" *What an awesome thought!*

"It was a perfectly natural thing to do. She respects, admires and loves you. Why *shouldn't* she name her baby after you?"

This has to be unreal, a dream! she thought. Why in the world would Barb choose to do this? "I've just done what I had to, Rob. Doesn't she know that?"

He'd reached over to the stand for tissues, and was wiping away tears she hadn't realized were starting down her cheeks. "Why should she? Gram and Gin and I—and lots of other people—don't know that, either!

"You've knocked yourself out taking care of things here, in addition to all your work responsibilities. And all this with Gram then Barb and now Jana—honestly, Van, how can you even say you've done all this from a sense of duty? You'll never convince any of us of that."

"I hadn't thought of it that way before." Her head fit against his shoulder as easily as though it had done this for years, and his arm around her gave her a wonderful sense of peace, of assurance. "I do love her, and all of them. I really do."

"I know...."

His cheek moved against the softness of her hair, that buckwheat-blond hair made lighter on top because of last summer's sun. The scent of her—so familiar, yet missed for so long—clean, wholesome, fresh-smelling, not cloyingly sweet or pungent or overwhelming.

He'd even gone out with women whose perfume got his sinuses acting up. "I'm glad you don't wear lots of perfume."

She turned enough to look into his eyes. "That's sort of a non sequitur, isn't it?"

"Not if you knew my thoughts."

"And I gather it's best for me not to know them?"

"Oh, I'd definitely like to share them with you—but when I do, I'd prefer that they be the only topic of our conversation, not in competition with what we *must* talk about—the funeral."

She looked at him for a long moment, and there was something in her eyes which made him wonder if this was the moment to speak more personally. I hate passing up this chance, he thought, but feel I have to. She snuggled back to where she'd been, and he told of things Barb had said to Gram, and to him.

"First of all, although she wants no notice of this in the paper, or anything fancy, she asks that it be held in the church. And she'd like whoever is there to sing "Jesus Loves Me" and "Jesus Loves the Children of the World," and also "He's Got the Whole World in His Hands" because, she told me, 'We sang that just last Sunday, and there's a verse in there about God's holding tiny children in his arms.'

"And she insists that the only flowers to be used should come from Gram's flower beds." He had to pause for a bit before going on, "I've already asked, at her request, for our pastor to serve, and of course he's agreed—and Lucy will play the organ."

He wondered if Vanessa might feel any resentment that they'd decided all these things without so much as talking it over with her—but she gave no indication of that when saying, "Thanks for taking care of things, Rob. I'm sure it will be a lovely funeral."

Remembering those days when she'd argued vehemently that there was no such thing as a *lovely funeral*, his lips brushed against her forehead as he murmured, "You're welcome."

She seemed content just sitting there, not even talking, until he whispered, "Are you going to sleep?"

She shifted enough to look into his eyes again, yet remain against him, his arm holding her there. "Not at the moment, but for the first time today I feel relaxed, at peace. I was thinking about Baby Vanessa, and *me* as a baby.

"I'd almost forgotten it but, a long time ago, Dad showed me the beautiful little long-skirted white dress he'd bought for me to wear when, as an infant, I was dedicated there at the front of our church. He took it from the drawer where he kept his undershirts, and carefully unwrapped the blue tissue paper from around it and held it up for me to see.

"I'm sorry to say that didn't mean much to me at the time, but later, sometimes when things in my life got very complicated, I held on to that memory as proof that he loved me so much that he still treasured that special baby dress.

"And I was wondering, Rob, if Barb would find that her baby's wearing my dress would make *her* feel as loved, as part of the family as it used to make me."

"Oh, Van!" He couldn't help it—he'd resolved to move slowly, to not risk frightening her off again this time by his too obvious love. But now he drew her into a bear hug—*a lover's hug,* he corrected himself. This time he kissed her on the lips, firmly, passionately—and was rewarded by the realization that she was responding, kissing him back! If only—dear God, if only…

It was Vanessa who finally broke the kiss, although she stayed in his embrace, face buried against his neck, breathing rapidly, almost panting. "I'm sorry…."

"Dear Vanessa, I will *never* be sorry for this night." He wanted to kiss her again—to kiss her forever—but she snuggled back into her previous position against his shoulder and he forced himself to not press her, to give the time she apparently needed.

It was a while later that she asked, "What do you think of my idea?"

For a moment he had to concentrate hard, for he'd obviously not been thinking similar thoughts. "About your little infant dress?" She nodded and he suggested, "It's a beautiful gesture on your part, but do you think you have the right to ask your father to part with it? It must mean even more to him than to you if he's still keeping it where you said—with his intimate apparel, the garments he wears closest to his heart."

Her look of surprise gradually changed into a sweet, somewhat tremulous smile. "I never thought of it in those terms. It *must* mean that."

She reached up, fingertips lightly caressing his lips. "You say such beautiful things, Rob—you have such beautiful thoughts. Thank you."

This time she shook her head just a little when he tried to pull her closer. "I have another idea, too, but *this* one I'm keeping to myself."

I wish you'd share it, but... "Afraid I'll dissuade you again? I really don't mean to be a wet blanket, Van."

"I know that! And I do appreciate your input, your insight. But I'm not sure I can pull this off."

"Anything I can do to help?" *I desperately want to be part of whatever you're doing, or even thinking about.*

"Not this time—not right now, anyway...."

It was with obvious reluctance that he left shortly after that, when Vanessa pleaded exhaustion. When she closed up for the night and climbed the stairs she stood in the hallway looking around at the four closed doors behind which Gram's girls were sleeping. Gram's girls—*her* girls as of now.

She started toward Gram's room, the one she'd been using ever since her grandmother's fall, but Barb's door, next to hers, was also open. She paused, glanced around again, and went inside, snapping on the light. In a way, she felt guilty checking out this room, as though she didn't trust Barb.

It was some time later when she finally entered her own room. She'd have to be in touch with Aunt Phyl, Gram and her mother first thing in the morning.

Morning seemed to come very soon, but Vanessa rolled over, turned off the alarm and got up. Considering everything, she was almost surprised, and grateful, to have slept as well as she did. She hoped, if Suz was free enough of her own responsibilities to help, to get the undone paperwork from last evening completed in short order once she got to work. *If* things went well, she'd try to make that other stop while on her so-called "break for lunch."

She had a number of interruptions, but the one most appreciated was Drew's stopping by for a few minutes before flying back to Chicago. He expressed regret at not being able to stay for Baby Vanessa's funeral, but had to fly to Hong Kong early the following morning.

"But look, Van, do get in touch with me if you need anything—anything at all, here or at Mary-jean's."

"I appreciate that, Drew, and so will Gram. Just

knowing you're available makes a tremendous difference.''

His hand rested on her shoulder. ''I'm proud we're in the same family, Vanessa McHenry—as well as being on the same team here.'' He gave her shoulder a firm squeeze—and was gone. She stood there staring at the door he'd closed behind himself and heard the deepness of his voice as he said farewell to Suz. Then all was quiet.

She made the phone call she'd almost dreaded, fearing the answer might be, ''There's not enough time.'' However, when she explained the urgency, the woman said to come immediately and she'd see what might be done.

She left at once and, already away from the office, made her necessarily brief visits with Gram and with Barb. Gram admitted that she'd shamelessly twisted arms and made all kinds of promises about keeping up with exercises and coming in twice next week for therapy, and was overjoyed at being allowed to go home the next day!

''I've already called Rob, and he's promised that the ramp will be taken care of tonight, for sure—and my bed and dresser will be waiting for me there in the dining room!''

''Great! Did you call home? Do the girls know?''

"Of course! I did that right after calling Rob."

"And you didn't even think to call me!" Vanessa pretended a pout, but Gram apparently knew her too well, for she laughed when her granddaughter stated, "Well you're stuck with me anyhow, so there!"

"Y'know something, Vanessa?" The laughter gradually left her face. "My fall was almost worth having just to get to know you so much better. I like very much what I'm seeing in you—what you are doing, and who you are."

"I consider that a special compliment, Gram, coming from you. Thanks." But then, because time was passing so quickly, she had to tell about last night and this morning. "And now I must share what I've done, and what I plan to do...."

Gram listened, and gave approval with two provisos: "Talk to Paula first, dear. Be sure you talk to your mother. And your dad."

Her father was one of the four men who showed up before Vanessa and the girls finished eating their evening meal. "I can't very well say, 'Just ignore us,' when we're sawing and hammering right outside your back door," Rob pseudo-apologized. "But we have to get this done, and

Jeff and Pete must go to the high school for something their kids are involved with.''

"No problem," Vanessa assured him, but had to insist that the girls finish eating and get things cleared away before going outside to watch and visit. She had stripped Gram's bed, and now asked if she should remove drawers from the dresser, so it could more easily be carried.

"And don't bother moving things in the dining room, either," Dad told her. "Just tell us how you want things rearranged and we'll get it done in no time."

She was grateful for this offer; the girls were probably strong enough to help, but she wanted no danger of any of *them* having difficulties with their pregnancies.

The bed was moved first, and Ricki and Kate volunteered to bring down fresh linens and bedspread and make it for her.

It wasn't long before they were finished. Dad and Rob stayed for ice cream and cookies after the others left for the school, and there was informal conversation and sharing. She was still waiting for an opportunity to have time alone with her father when he glanced at the clock on the electric stove. "Wow! Look at the time." He got to his feet and came over to give her a hug. "Thanks for saving the fort, kid."

It's been a long time—too long a time since you've called me "kid." "Gram has built a strong fort, Dad. Even this second line of defense could keep it going."

"So *you* say." And he kissed her.

She walked with him out the back door and to where his car was parked near the garage. She couldn't have asked for a better time, a better opportunity to talk with him about the funeral. And of other things.

Rob had gathered his tools and put them in his car. He should already be home, changed into his suit, and joining Elmer for tonight's viewing, but hated to leave until he had at least a minute or two with Van. She, however, seemed to be in some serious conversation with her father, so he said his farewells to the girls and walked toward his vehicle.

He'd have to content himself with the single fingerstroke along Van's arm as he passed them, and with their smiling response to his, "Have a good night!"

He'd parked just behind Brad, so now raised his hand and smiled at him and his daughter as he drove by. I wonder if their discussion is about what Van hesitated to speak of last night. How I wish she'd have shared it with me! he thought.

But then he thought again of that kiss, that passionate kiss which had so filled him with joy. And hope! He was still smiling as he drove home.

Chapter Fourteen

"I'm sorry to bother you again tonight, Mother, when you're so busy."

Paula McHenry had come in and kicked off her designer pumps as she sat down in Gram's favorite rocker. "I realize you can't leave here in the evening."

"Well, I promised Gram to talk to you about two things I planned to do tomorrow—but I won't go through with it if you'd rather I didn't."

"Ah, this sounds intriguing." The slight smile on her lips didn't quite make it to her eyes. "What do you have in mind?"

"Well—I'm not even going to try making this long story short, if you don't mind." Receiving a nod, she told of Barb's finding the doll in the attic here, and how she'd immediately latched on to it. "I'd forgotten it, although I understand it used to belong to me."

There was a tightness around her mother's lips, and her eyes seemed to narrow a bit when Vanessa added, "And I believe you gave it to me."

"Yes. I did give it to you."

"I must not have been very old, perhaps four or five?"

"You were four. I was away at a convention when I bought that doll for your birthday. It was quite expensive for me at that stage of my career." There was a momentary pause. "You did not want it."

"I can't remember ever playing with dolls. Did I?"

"Oh, you had an old raggedy cloth one Gram brought down from her attic...."

"I may *vaguely* remember that."

"But I wanted you to have a *pretty* doll," Paula said, "one you could take anywhere, even to church."

"Did we go to church together back then?" *I probably shouldn't go off on sidetracks like this, but...*

"Once in a while, like when you had a part in some Sunday School performance, or at Christmas."

I'm glad to be reminded of that—but must get back to the doll. "So you brought me the baby doll for my fourth birthday...."

"That was so long ago, Vanessa. Why bother about it now?"

"There seems to be something *there*, something I should be remembering."

Mother drew in a deep breath as she sat up more erectly in that chair which had not rocked at all. "You were here at Gram's when I got back, on the front sidewalk, so I came to you and held out the doll, saying something like, 'I brought you this gorgeous baby for your birthday.'

"But you didn't even reach for it, just said— and these are your exact words, I'll never forget them—'But I wanted *you* for my birthday.'

"I explained again that I was very busy and that it was often necessary for me to be away. And then I again tried to hand you the doll."

She paused, but this time Vanessa was not about to ask anything which might somehow keep her from learning what she was beginning to think must have a lot to do with—with *what?* Their relationship?

"You grabbed it by the legs and threw it down right here on Gram's front sidewalk. I was so angry that I yelled at you for being such an ungrateful, destructive child, and reached out without thinking, and slapped you across the face.''

She did now recall something about that—the only time she knew of when her mother punished her physically.

''You started crying, turned and ran up the steps and into the house, and I leaned over and picked up that doll, which now had a broken head. I said something about the *poor baby,* and it was then—'' she paused, and Vanessa saw tears in her eyes ''—your father said, with a bitterness I'll never forget, 'Did you think you're the only female in the family who has the right to destroy babies?'

''And he turned and walked away.''

Vanessa stared at her mother, sitting there with tears running down her cheeks. She'd never seen her cry before, and had no idea what to say or do other than reach out to take her hand.

''And I had no answer to give.''

The cosmetic blush her mother had so artfully applied stood out against her blanched face. ''It's time you knew, Vanessa. You think I've done something selfless and good in trying to help those girls upstairs—and Barb...''

Vanessa's voice was gentle as she reminded, ''Not many lawyers would have freely given all that knowledge and wisdom and *time* to save the lives of these babies, and to help them.''

"But it was your father, not I, who saved *you*."

Those words were spoken so softly that she could hardly believe what she heard. "What?"

"Law school is unbelievably difficult, Vanessa. Brad and I were so much in love that we got married earlier than we should have—and weren't as careful as we intended to be.

"I was horrified to find myself pregnant right there in our first year—but I *couldn't* tell Brad. With that apparently inbred McHenry love of family and children, he probably would have been *happy* about it! So I had an abortion—which he was never to know about.

"We were both doing well in school, though I was a little jealous of its seeming to come easier for him. I had to work *extremely* long hours and was exhausted much of the time, yet needed sleeping pills to get what rest I did.

"It was almost two years later when I again became pregnant—with you."

This pause was so long that Vanessa was trying to think of something—*anything* to say when her mother picked up the account. "Brad came in and found me throwing up and crying. Instantly solicitous—you know how caring he can be—he held me in his arms, wanting to know what was wrong.

"And I blurted out that I was pregnant again."

Vanessa reached for both of her hands, but said nothing.

"So that's when he found out that I planned to—to do what I'd done before. He was insistent that I go through with the pregnancy, and I was sure I couldn't keep up with my classes, as miserable as I was. He made me promise not to have the abortion—and was horrified that I'd done it before, without giving him input on what he called the murder of his baby.

"Actually, with his coaching me through much of that long period when I was so nauseated, I did make out okay." She freed one perfectly manicured hand and pushed it back through her hair. "But then you were born—and what a fussy, crying infant you were!"

"I'm so sorry...."

"Oh, it wasn't your fault—I'm not blaming you for feeling as rotten as you must have been, but we took you to doctor after doctor and tried everything they suggested, and even some of the old wives' tales or remedies. From being in the top third of the class, I almost failed that semester, even with Brad taking over more and more of your care. Then he dropped out the next semester...."

"In order to care for *me?*"

"Yes, to care for you." She got up and started pacing. "It was supposed to be for just the one semester, two at the most—and then he'd pick up where he'd left. But one thing happened, then another. He began drinking—which I could not tolerate—and that drove us yet farther apart.''

''But you stayed together....''

''We continued living in the same house.''

No wonder I saw no loving touches, no secret smiles across the room, none of the things which seemed to take place all the time between Gram and Grandad. This time when she whispered, ''I'm sorry,'' it was not an apology for things she might have done even unintentionally; it was abject sorrow, a sadness for all these years of cool correctness to which her parents had subjected themselves.

Mother came back to the rocker and sat down, face and manner again almost as cool and composed as usual. ''What was it you wished to talk about with me?''

''Well, I've been thinking of having that doll repaired, and giving it to Barb—she has taken quite a fancy to it.''

Paula shrugged. ''It's yours, Vanessa. You have every right to do with it as you like.''

''I'm—not sure I want to now, not with what you've just told me.''

There was the sound of a short laugh, but Mother was not seeing humor in this. ''Don't keep

it because you think I want you to. I had thrown
it in the garbage. I was *most* surprised to see Barb
with it the other day.''

"But if you threw it away..." Vanessa realized
what must have taken place. "Gram saw—and res-
cued it!"

"She must have—" Paula nodded "—and took
it to the attic, with all those many other 'treasures'
she can't bear to throw away."

"And the doll's dress? Did that come with it?"

Paula frowned as she strained to think back all
those years. "It must have. There was no reason
to get clothes for it later...."

Vanessa didn't mention the doll to her father
when he called midmorning to say he'd brought
Gram home. She'd made out fine using the walker
on the ramp and was even staying in the kitchen
to have a cup of tea with her girls. Her idea of
moving the master chair from the dining room had
worked very well, its sturdy walnut arms offering
good support in getting back on her feet.

Vanessa said she'd happened to think of her little dedication dress which he'd once shown her,
and wondered if she might see it again. She was
grateful he didn't ask why she wanted this, and he
agreed with her suggestion that she stop there for
a few minutes on the way home.

She walked upstairs with him and sat on his bed in his very masculine room. Going directly to that same neatly arranged drawer, he shifted undershirts from the left side so he could remove the flat, elongated packet.

Laying it on the bed beside her, he carefully unfolded the blue tissue wrappings and stood there silently looking down at the delicate white lace, the ribbons, the sweetheart neckline and the full, long skirt.

"It's so beautiful, Dad! Where did you find it?"

"I'd gone to Philadelphia with a friend, and we stopped at a mall on the way back. He was checking to see if some store still carried a special something he'd once found there, so we decided to meet back at the car in thirty or forty minutes.

"As you know, I do *not* enjoy shopping, so was just meandering along, looking in windows, when I passed a maternity-and-baby shop. *This,*" he said, indicating the dress, "was on a doll in the window, and it seemed so dainty and delicate and *pure* that I had to get it for you—even though the clerks weren't happy about that."

He gave a crooked smile, remembering. "It turned out they had only one of these—and wanted it left on display. However, there *was* a price tag on it and it was in the window, so I insisted on speaking to the manager. And bought it for my beautiful, wonderful baby daughter.''

His gaze rose to meet hers, and there was a genuine, sweet smile on his lips and in his eyes as he added, ''Perhaps it's foolish, and you may not appreciate my saying this right now, but I'm hoping that some day you'll marry someone truly worthy of you, and that the two of you have a daughter.

''Maybe this little dress will be worn again....''

She stood up and slipped her arms around him, and he hugged her close. ''If I do marry and have a daughter, Dad, I now know where to come for an absolutely perfect little dedication dress.''

Vanessa could hardly wait to welcome Gram and Barb from the hospital, but as she hurried in the back door she was aware of a strange quietness. AnnaMae had her finger up in front of her lips. ''Shhh. Barb's sleeping on the couch, and Gram's asleep, too.''

''What about the others?'' She was looking around. ''Where *is* everyone?''

''Andi was here until a few minutes ago, and when she walked home she asked if someone would come with her to bring back the roast she'd put in her slow cooker.

''Jana's still afraid to walk back alone, even that little way....''

"I don't want *any* of you alone right now," she reminded.

"The others wanted to go, anyway."

"Did they say when they'd be back?"

"Just that they wouldn't stay long."

Vanessa went upstairs to change clothes, and as she came back down saw Rob coming up the front porch steps. "Welcome," she greeted, opening the door and going outside.

"Why are you whispering?" His volume matched hers.

"We have a couple of 'sleeping beauties' in there, Gram in her bed and Barb on the couch."

"That condition must be epidemic," he said dryly. "I had a brief sleep, too—after being up most of the night."

She'd heard there had been a car accident last night, but didn't know either of the young people who had been involved. "I used to know the driver's mother when I was a child, but I haven't seen much of her since." She then asked if Rob's mortuary had the funeral for the girl who had died.

"No, we don't. And, in case you wondered, that is *not* why I'm an EMT and go on ambulance calls."

She stared up at him, shocked at his thinking that a possibility. "Never in my wildest dreams could I imagine you being after business in that way—that you are an *accident chaser!*''

His smile was a little crooked. "I didn't mean to imply that I thought that you thought..."

Their being so careful about one another's feelings suddenly seemed funny and she laughed. It was only a split second later that his arm came around her and he was chuckling, too. "I think we'd make out a lot better if we talked *straight* to each other."

She thrust out her hand. "It's a deal! No making assumptions nor skirting issues."

"That's one fantastic deal!" He solemnly shook her hand, and continued holding it. "And, if we're to be that open and honest, perhaps this is the time for me to tell you that I love you."

Her quick intake of air was almost a gasp. *A profession of love here on Gram's porch in broad daylight? But why not...?* "That—I wasn't expecting that, Rob," she stammered. "But—thank you."

"I didn't mean to make you uneasy...."

She drew in a deliberately long breath. "And we're doing it again, aren't we?"

He smiled down into her eyes. "Old traits die hard."

"Yes." How well she knew this! "Very hard."

But they had no time or opportunity to continue

in this vein, for Kate was running ahead of the other girls, waving something in her hand. "Wait till you see these! Andi took instantly developed pictures of us with Baby Katherine. Aren't they *neat?*"

She shoved them in front of Vanessa, bubbling over with the news that Andi had let her hold the baby. "...And I even got to change her diaper!"

That was not at the top of Vanessa's can't-wait-to-do list, but she still rejoiced at not only Kate's delight with the photographs, but also Ricki's— and especially Jana's!

However, seeing the dainty little outfit on Katherine reminded her of still not having made provision for a dress for Barb's infant. But then Rob said, "I came to ask advice from all you lovely ladies."

Vanessa was almost amused at how seriously the others responded, but then she, too, became involved as he said he had a suggestion, but didn't know how it would be taken. "You already know about the coffin we're using for the baby, but someone came in today with a special gift for her."

"Who's it from?" Kate asked.

"That's the one thing I can't tell you, for it's to be kept anonymous. But I'd like to show it to you, so you can help decide how to present it to Barb."

Vanessa had, of course, noticed the plain white

box he'd been carrying under his arm, but now he laid it on the wicker table between two of the porch chairs, opened it, and folded back the white tissue. It was Jana who reached for it, lifting it by the shoulder seams. "Oh, Vanessa, you bought it! Thank you for…"

Vanessa put her arm around the girl standing there beaming at her. "No, dear, I had nothing at all to do with this. I did consider it, and would have liked to, but didn't."

"Well, *some*one did, that's for sure," Ricki exclaimed.

"Is this the same one you saw at the store?"

"Yes." The affirmation was little more than a breath. "I'm positive it's the same perfect little dress."

I wonder if Mother could have done this. That hardly seemed possible, for if there was anyone who didn't believe in encouraging someone's misdeeds, it was she. But who else would know the importance of this one special garment? Who could have bought it? Did Mrs. Holtzmaier, at the store, regret turning Jana in to the police? Could Gram have decided to do it? Or Gin? Andi? Her father…?

She was so involved with these possibilities that she lost track of the conversation for a moment.

Jana was saying, "Just tell her what you told us. I know she'll be pleased."

AnnaMae had joined them by now. "Isn't it great that whoever it is doesn't want us to know? Just think—wherever Barb goes, whoever she sees, she has to wonder if maybe *that's* the person who cares so much."

"*I'd* like to know if it was me," Jana stated. "I'd want to thank her—or him, wouldn't you?"

Vanessa wanted to say she agreed with AnnaMae, but she suspected Rob had deliberately asked the girls so they'd have to think things through. Kate surprised her with, "Probably the best way she or *any* of us can thank that person is to become the best we can. You know, get to be like the person who gave this."

Vanessa felt Rob's gaze before she met it. There was joy there, pure unadulterated happiness—and she felt like that, too. Sometimes she'd wondered, in those times of exhaustion and being almost overwhelmed both at work and here, if all this effort was worth it, if they were getting anywhere at all.

But yes! Not only had it been *worth* it, but she felt assured that these girls were developing into fine young women! And she'd been privileged to have a part in it!

Chapter Fifteen

⟡

They had prayers together around Gram's bed that night, then the five girls went on upstairs. Vanessa had determined not to ask even Gram about the little dress, but now Gram was asking her, "Was it *you?*"

She shook her head, then told about AnnaMae's and Kate's reasoning. "I'm going to keep trying to be as wise as they are, Gram. How can I dislike or be suspicious of *anyone,* if he or she could be the person responsible for this?"

Gram nodded agreement, then asked, "Was it *awfully* hard on Barb when you drove her to the funeral home this evening?"

"Not as bad as I feared. She cried, of course— and she'll never be able to put this totally behind her." She felt unbidden tears again forming as she added, "I—believe she's now accepted the fact that the baby's dead—and that her own life must go on...."

But when she went upstairs later, Barb's door was open and the light still on. "Are you okay, dear?" Vanessa asked.

Barb was lying across her bed, and had obviously been crying. "Can I ask you something?"

"Of course." Vanessa sat on the bed beside her, hand rubbing the girl's back. "You may ask anything."

"What's to become of me?"

She wasn't prepared for this—not now, right before the funeral. But first of all she'd better be certain as to what that question pertained. "What do you mean?"

"I'm—not pregnant anymore. And my baby will be buried tomorrow. Do I have to leave right away? Like—tomorrow?"

"Oh, Barb!" She leaned over and drew the girl into her embrace. She felt so little, so frail, so—in despair. "No, dear, you do *not* have to leave tomorrow! Not for a long, long time."

"But when I have to leave, where will I go? I can't return to Mom's...not with *him*—or some other guy there!"

"Believe me, Barb, you will *never* have to go

there." With everything else, she'd neglected to talk over with this child-woman what she knew about the police investigation, so did some of that now. There were many things she herself didn't know, but just talking about it seemed to make Barb less fearful.

By the time Vanessa said, "I really must get some sleep," Barb said she was drowsy, too.

Funeral day. Vanessa's mind registered that before her eyes even opened, and she burrowed her head under the pillow. She did not like funerals; she never did and never would! There was too much finality....

She opened one eye and squinted at the clock. It was still ten minutes before the alarm would ring, but she turned it off and got up. She'd get her shower right away, then go down and mix up a batch of blueberry muffins—or perhaps waffles, to be eaten with maple syrup or jelly.

She was shampooing her hair before she admitted to herself that her sudden desire for domesticity was primarily an escape from thinking of what would soon be taking place.

Gram was awake when she got downstairs, but Vanessa talked the older woman into staying in bed until she brought tea to the dining-bedroom for both of them. "It's going to be a beautiful day."

Gram was looking toward the window. "I'm grateful for that. A rainy funeral makes it seem like the whole world's crying."

"Gram...has Barb asked you about the baby dying like this? About if Baby Vanessa could possibly be in heaven?"

"I assured her that was the case. I have no doubts at all that she'll be waiting for us there." Her voice was clear and positive, even though they were keeping their volume low.

"That came up when we talked last night. One of her biggest concerns right now is wondering if *she'll* get there to be with her baby."

"I must spend more time with her." Gram took another sip of her tea. "I regret that I wasn't here to help her through most of this."

"And I'm sorry I couldn't do a better job."

"I don't want to hear one more word about that, Vanessa!" Gram shook her head, frowning her remonstration. "You did very, *very* well."

She wasn't going to argue, even though she still wished she'd done more. "I'm planning on blueberry muffins for breakfast."

"Good! They all like them, and so do I...."

She'd got out the ingredients, but did not make the muffins right away, for the girls, having been told last night they could sleep in as long as they'd like, straggled down throughout the next hour. Most were still in pajamas or nightgowns, but Barb was already wearing the relatively full-cut dark-blue dress in which she'd arrived in Sylvan Falls months ago, before needing maternity clothes.

They sat around the kitchen table after they'd finished eating, reheating their tea or refilling their glasses with orange juice, milk or water. No one mentioned the baby or the funeral until, after glancing at the clock, Gram stated, ''I must get washed and dressed, or I'll make everyone late.''

Rob came for them in the limousine, and helped Gram into the front with him. Vanessa, sitting in the center of the back seat with Barb and Jana, tried not to compare this with that previous occasion when they had ridden in this vehicle. She couldn't help recalling what a good time they'd had, and she heard Kate and Ricki whispering about it.

Rob assisted Gram out at the foot of the ramp leading to the front door of the church, and they all went in that way while one of the part-time helpers drove the vehicle away, presumably to have it in proper position for taking them to the cemetery following the service.

Lucy Ammand was already there, playing soft

organ music which sounded vaguely familiar and classical, but Vanessa didn't even try to remember what it was.

Gram led the way up the aisle, taking her time with her walker to the small, white-satin-lined, marbleized casket. It was on a draped table, and all seven of them, Gram, the five girls and Vanessa, stood there in a semicircle, looking down at the little one. "She looks like she's just asleep," Jana whispered.

Kate nodded, and Vanessa hugged her as the young woman struggled with trying to keep from crying.

"That hat looks real nice on Baby Vanessa," Barb whispered. "Thanks, Jana, for thinking of it."

There was activity at the back of the sanctuary, and Vanessa realized that Andi, Keith and Katherine had arrived, as did more of the extended family, and also a great many people from church.

"I've been praying for you, dear—many of us have, and we're going to keep right on doing so." Miz Aggie had come up to Barb, and was holding her close. "I'm sad that things worked out this way, but I'm sure God's going to bless you in unexpected but wonderful ways...."

The president of the PTA and the assistant principal of the school came, as well as Aunt Phyl and

Uncle Hal, and Aunt Shelby and Uncle Zack. Dad arrived alone, and it was nearly time for the service to begin when Vanessa's mother got there. She stood by the casket for a long time, and Vanessa moved over to be there with her. Somehow it felt *right* to put an arm around her mother's waist, and to whisper, "It's almost over."

Her mother shook her head. "No. Not yet."

Not being sure what that referred to, Vanessa remained silent, and her mother added, "The police now have Roger Hamstead—and his red car with the broken window.

"Rob was authorized to take hair clippings from the baby, which we may still need for DNA testing to prove that man raped Barb, that he fathered her child."

Vanessa shivered, feeling chilled—yet angry. "Will he be up for murder, for the baby's death?"

"I'm not sure we can make that stick—but for raping a minor, and for the *attempted* murder of Barb—yes, I believe we've got the witnesses and evidence to prove that."

Pastor Harriman had come to speak with them, but Vanessa didn't see him again until after Rob unobtrusively said it was time for them to take their places in the front pews. When she was seated and looked again, the diminutive coffin had been closed.

Barb gave a little sob, and leaned against Gram's shoulder for a bit before sitting up straight again, her right hand holding tightly onto Vanessa's.

Their minister was wearing a black suit and tie, as if this were a "usual" service, but instead of being up at the pulpit he remained on the same level as the people gathered together for their farewell to the baby. He used scripture passages Vanessa had heard at funerals before, but the one meaning the most to her was Jesus' saying, "Today you will be with me in Paradise."

He used the analogy of a dragonfly as it changed from one form to another in its lifetime to indicate that Baby Vanessa, although unable to survive in this life, would now have a strong, healthy body with God.

But his speaking about love was when the message hit her hardest, making her thoughts go off on their own. Barb's love for her little daughter, right from the beginning—love's demanding personal sacrifice—love's being tough and long-lasting.

He said that the baby's mother had asked that everyone sing several of the songs she would have liked to teach her daughter, but which she hoped would also be meaningful to each person here. So Lucy played and they sang "Jesus Loves Me"— and the words stirred Vanessa's heart. *Did* He? *Could* He? Well, the Bible does say that's so....

And then there was, "Jesus Loves the Little Children," and it *did* seem possible He could love all the children of the world. She couldn't really fathom it—but that didn't mean a thing. A month ago it would have been inconceivable that Vanessa McHenry would come to love these five girls so much that her heart was breaking for Barb—and for Jana—and for the future of each of them.

And, even more surprising, she had come to love Rob! Dad had said he hoped she'd marry a man worthy of her—but Rob was far beyond worthy of her, he was so loving and caring and giving....

And he'd told her yesterday that he loved her.

It was almost unbelievable that he was in love with *her,* with all her drive for professionalism and advancement, with her innate selfishness....

But she was woolgathering here at Baby Vanessa's funeral, of all places! She was, indeed, unworthy of someone like Rob.

They were now singing all the verses of the old spiritual, "He's Got the Whole World in His Hands." There was the verse with "...the wind and the rain," and then "He's got the tiny little baby in His hands..." By then she was incapable of singing the last verse, except in her mind and heart: "...you and me, brother..."

It was true that she didn't understand all of what was said in church, and she'd never read the Bible as much as she had since coming to Gram's, but at that moment she had the certainty that God truly did have this tiny little baby, Vanessa Barbara Mutchler, in His hands—and in His Heaven, wherever that was and whatever it was like.

She looked around, and everything was different. The sun was shining through the stained glass windows of the sanctuary just as before, but it *seemed* brighter, clearer and more illuminating.

She found herself sitting straighter in the pew and releasing Barb's hand, but giving it a pat of encouragement. The service was over, and those people in the front pews were allowed to remain where they were until the others had the opportunity to leave.

And then, because Barb had asked for the privilege of doing this, she started to carry the diminutive coffin out to the hearse. Vanessa walked beside her, realizing that the burden was heavier than it looked, both physically and emotionally; the baby in this little casket contained many of the hopes and dreams of her mother, and of those who loved her.

Barb almost stumbled, and Vanessa reached to help her. She'd never been a pallbearer before—would never have dreamed she'd be—but it was a way she could share Barb's burden of loss. She would do far more than this for love.

The ride in the limousine. The brief committal service. The ride back to the church, where a meal had been prepared and was now served. Vanessa had thought she didn't want to do this, either. Yet the fellowship, far more than the food, strengthened the girls—and her.

Rob had mentioned that he and Elmer were frequently invited to join family and friends following a funeral, so it was no surprise when he sat across the table from her and Barb, and his partner was across from Gram.

There were several long tables of those staying, perhaps fifty or sixty people, maybe more, but she wasn't curious enough to count. AnnaMae and Jana had remained near them, but Kate and Ricki were sitting with Karlyn. After what appeared to be a slow start, they seemed to be involved in conversation.

Everyone was about finished with the meal when it struck Vanessa that she'd not even thought about the office—about things at work—all day! It was a shock to realize this; she'd been driven by the "work ethic" all her adult life, so this seemed strange.

Gram had gone over to thank the church women who'd worked in the kitchen and served the meal, and Vanessa did likewise a little later. It's only proper to do so, she told herself—but knew she wanted to let them know how much she appreciated them. What they did today and what some had done as to preparing food during the time Gram was in the hospital was *very* much appreciated.

Many at work had asked how things were going and had commiserated with her, but only Suz, unable to be here today, had made any real effort to help.

Why did it take the death of an innocent baby to make me wake up, God? I must be so very dense....

Rob had been talking with Gram and now came over to ask, "Might it be time to get your grandmother back home?"

"She wouldn't admit it, but she's undoubtedly exhausted." She looked toward Gram and smiled. "Isn't she amazing?"

"It must run in the family."

She wanted to respond to that, but this wasn't the time. "I'll go round up the girls."

"So that leaves *me* with the hard part—trying to get Gram to go home before every last person does."

She laughed for what may have been the first time this day. "If you succeed, this should go down in the record books!"

But the older woman must have been even more worn out than they'd guessed, for she made no objections—and the girls, too, were more than ready. Once in the limousine, all but Barb were trying to talk at once. Neither Gram nor Vanessa made any effort to interrupt or to ask them to quiet down.

Rob had not expected Vanessa to go along with everything so readily. In school she'd always been a leader, coming up with more ideas in less time than anyone he knew—and usually getting classmates to go along with them!

When she discovered that seventh-graders couldn't sing in the high school's mixed chorus, she engineered a group, the Seventh Grade Singers, which was so good they got called on a number of times during that year—and the following year became the Eighth Grade Angels!

And as a senior she became the year book editor by sheer determination, creating special features which won the support of the faculty—and led to one of the most outstanding volumes the school had, at least until then, ever published.

This woman who had not been interested in having a family of her own, who had prided herself on being sufficient unto herself, had held together the household when Gram was no longer there, giving more of herself than she'd realized she had to give.

And now she was sitting back there with the girls and he was up in the front with Gram who, most untypically, was not talking much, probably too fatigued to do so. He looked into the rearview mirror, but was unable to catch Vanessa's eye. He couldn't hear what she was saying, either, but those in the middle seats had partially turned in order to be in the conversation.

Please, Lord, help me have the opportunity to speak with her alone. Give me the right words and help me put them together in the best way—and let her hear them and know how much I love her.

I think she loves me, too, but is there enough love that she'll be able to respond in like manner to my profession of devotion? She's come so far in reaching out to and helping others—is it selfish on my part to ask that You continue helping her see that it's okay to acknowledge and accept my love, as well as give hers to me...?

They were back at the house, and he ached to help Gram as, with the walker, she made her slow way up the ramp, into the house and to her bed. The girls carried in containers of salads, macaroni and cheese, baked limas, pickled eggs, cold meats and desserts which the church women had sent home with them.

Vanessa said she'd find room in the refrigerator for these while they went up to change clothes, and Rob assisted her in transferring some of the foods into smaller containers, grateful for these unhurried moments together.

They spoke of how well Barb had got through this difficult time, and of the pastor's message and the simple but meaningful committal service at the cemetery. They mentioned how difficult it would be for Jana to go back to school on Monday, and that Barb would be allowed to remain home for a couple of days if she asked to.

Vanessa found room for the very last container, closed the refrigerator door, and reached out both hands, palms up. "I have no words eloquent enough to tell you how much I appreciate all you've done for us—and for me—during this en-

tire time since Gram's accident. *Especially* for
these past several days. Thanks, Rob, for being
you."

He moved closer, taking her hands in his, holding them against his chest. "You're welcome, dear,
for anything I've done." He ventured a somewhat
hesitant smile as he looked down into those magnificent eyes. "Perhaps this isn't the right time to
tell you that you are also welcome to all that I am
now or ever may be.

"In other words, I am humbly asking you to
become my wife, my helpmate, the completion of
me, and of *you*—our becoming one...."

He'd hoped she'd rush into his arms, that they
would hold one another and kiss passionately, but
she drew in a startled gasp, and there was something in her eyes that looked as though she was
about to smile. "You took it literally when we
agreed to be totally honest with one another, didn't
you, Rob?"

He nodded, more serious than ever in his life,
but now fearing that he may have spoken prema-
turely. "I did, Vanessa. And I do."

And then she was in his arms, hers circling him
as tightly as his around her. But the kiss he'd been
anticipating had to wait as she whispered, "And I
do, too." She leaned backward against the support

of his arms so she could look into his eyes. "I love you, too, more than I ever dreamed I was capable of loving anyone."

"You have so much love to give...."

"I now believe you are right. But I didn't know that before...."

They went to the dining room and found Gram still awake. Beaming up at the happy couple, she asked, "You didn't really think I'd be surprised, did you?"

"Of *course* we did," Vanessa told her. "I didn't know myself how much I loved him."

And Gram shook her head. "Correction, my dear...you wouldn't *admit* to yourself that you were in love."

"And I didn't know for sure that she loved me, either, Gram. So all I could do was step out in *hope*, even if I was weak in faith."

"Well," Gram said, trying to readjust the pillow under her head and shoulders, "all I can say is that it's about time you two realized what I've known for at *least* the last week!"

Vanessa helped smooth the support, challenging, "So what else do you know that we should be made aware of?"

Gram's eyes were sparkling and she no longer

Eileen Berger 241

appeared to be at all sleepy. "You think I'm going to spoil even one of the surprises God has in store for you? No *way*, as the girls would put it!" Then she paused and looked from one to the other. "But I do have a favor to ask. May I please be present when you tell them that you're going to be married soon?"

"We didn't say anything about *soon*, Gram," Vanessa told her at the same time Rob was saying, "The sooner the better!"

"See?" Gram shrugged. "You're finding out some of the surprises already! Isn't this fun?"

Chapter Sixteen

Vanessa asked for perhaps an hour before telling the girls, saying she had a very important errand that had to be taken care of right away—a previous appointment which must be kept.

Gram fretted, "You don't have to go to the office *today,* do you?"

She assured them this was not the case so, although obviously curious, they said no more about it. She was carrying an oblong package when she returned, and asked everyone to come into the dining room. "Barb," she still wasn't quite sure how to say this, "I don't know whether this is the best time to give you what's in this box, but I hope it is.

"It's something you liked very much, but I

couldn't give it to you for a number of reasons—
my faulty memory, something I was ashamed of,
the lack of its perfection and my own selfishness.

"But the memory is now restored and my guilt
has been at least partially removed. And, as of right
now, even the lack of perfection has been taken
care of."

She looked around at the puzzled faces, especially Barb's. Only Gram was smiling, and Vanessa wondered if there was any possible way she
might have guessed this—or if she just might have
enough confidence in her granddaughter to trust
that what was about to take place was good. "Barbara, dear, I'd like you to open it."

The girl looked from the kraft-paper-wrapped
package to Vanessa and back again before pulling
off the first, then the rest of the tape strips securely
fastening it together. Folding back the covering
from the foot-and-a-half-long box, she lifted the
cover.

There was a gasp, a startled, speechless look upward, and then her hands gently lifted up the doll
she'd found in Gram's attic. "Oh, Vanessa!"
There was awe in her voice, a breathlessness un-
common to her. "She's perfect now...."

Vanessa went to her, placing one arm around the
rounded shoulders as she reached to touch the
doll's head, which no longer showed the slightest

blemish. "I was only four and very angry with my mother at the time she gave me this doll. In my hurt and resentment, I deliberately tried to destroy it, and only Gram's rescuing it from the garbage can made it possible for you to find it in the attic."

She smiled at Barb. "I recently called a woman who has a doll hospital and she agreed to repair the damage I'd done. So now, *finally,* this doll will belong to someone who truly loves her."

"I—loved her even before she belonged to me," Barb murmured, "before she was repaired."

"How like God that is!" Gram's voice was no louder than Barb's. "He loves us with all our imperfections."

Vanessa saw Gram's joy—and also that on the face of the man she loved. She went to him, and was filled with that same feeling as his arms encircled her, pulling her tightly back against his strong, warm body. "Would *you...?*" she asked, tilting sideways enough to look up at him.

He smiled down at her, then turned to the five girls, who all looked somewhat confused. "We have an announcement, which didn't surprise Gram at all, and *may* not you, either, although we thought it would.

"Vanessa and I are very much in love, and we plan to be married."

Even Barb forgot the doll in the excitement

which ensued. When would they be married?
Where would they live? They'd be having a big,
fancy wedding, wouldn't they? Would Vanessa
continue with her excellent position....?

Laughing, they explained that most of the many
questions could not yet be answered. "But you'll
be the first to know when our decisions are made,"
Vanessa assured them.

"It's strange," she admitted as she sat with Rob
on the porch swing after the others were in bed for
the night. "I'm the one who's always had to have,
right up front, the answer to every problem. But
this is different...."

He kissed her again—couldn't seem to get
enough of her lips. "This is, indeed, much different, sweetheart! It's far beyond developing new
electronic circuitry or an educational game—and
you aren't responsible for profit-and-loss reports
from and to department heads or to Drew and
Andi."

She nodded, head against his comfortable, sup-
porting shoulder. "Our accountability is to one another, right?"

"And to God."

Yes, that too. They would continue to have
questions, not only now but after their wedding—
perhaps *more* then, for all she knew. But they'd

handle them and work them out together, which would make all the difference in the world.

What will it be like if we have children? Vanessa thought of Rob sitting at Gram's table with the girls, and smiled. "I do love you with all my heart, Robert Corland."

"And I adore you, Vanessa...."

Epilogue

Graduation day was never treated lightly in Sylvan Falls, but this year was extraspecial for Vanessa, and for Gram's household. Both Barb and Jana had done very well during the second semester, making up for some of the problems during the first part of their school year.

"It seems," Gram said from her second-row seat in the stadium, saved for her by the newlyweds, Vanessa and Rob, "as though everyone in town is here!" She was holding Jana's four-month-old son, Michael, and Kate, Ricki, and AnnaMae had also insisted on bringing their little girls, Deborah, Candace, and Mary.

"It wouldn't seem right at all," AnnaMae had insisted, "for our little ones to miss out on being present for Aunt Barb's and Aunt Jana's graduation! There's no way they'll remember, but I think they'll be glad to know they were here.''

Vanessa had been afraid that one or more of the three older girls might feel she'd missed something important in not having had an official graduation ceremony like this, but there had been only gratitude for the opportunity to get their GEDs.

Vanessa and Andi, with the help of their husbands and Karlyn, had taken all five of the young women to every college and university in the area. Four of them were now, largely financed through available governmental programs, enrolled in baccalaureate programs, but Barb was more interested in the two-year food services program at the technical institute.

They were still living with Gram, and would continue scheduling such household duties as food preparation, cleaning, shopping and laundry, along with caring for the little ones, even after beginning college in the fall. In preparation for that, several of them were looking forward to taking courses this summer.

''They're coming!'' someone shouted as the band began to play, leading the procession from the high school's gymnasium out across the emerald grass to the rows of chairs. The speakers and honor students were first, even before those in administration, the school board members and the faculty. And then came the rest of the graduates, those who'd successfully completed their secondary education.

"There's Jana!" Vanessa cried, pointing.

Ricki squinted, struggling to distinguish the other face in the too-similar black gowns and flat-topped caps. "And Barb!"

Vanessa's heart was overflowing with happiness. It's true that some of Gram's and her original goals had not been attained, but oh, how much better the Master's plan had been! Although one of the babies died before birth and none of the others had been put up for adoption, here this day were five wonderful young adults with the whole world open before them.

Each had grown and developed and responded to Gram's love, and to the love of others—especially God's.

The speeches went smoothly, the music was lovely—and then came the presentation of diplomas. Yes! Jana was the next in line—was now a graduate! Baby Michael burped, wriggled a little and relaxed back against Gram, as though the important part of the evening was over now that his mother had received that paper.

Then Barb was given hers. *Thank you, Father, for being with them, with all our girls. We so ap-*

*preciate Your entrusting us with giving the love
and security and help they needed.*

Listening to the joyful sounds around her, Vanessa smiled. Other families had also undoubtedly found it necessary to work through serious problems and trials before arriving at this day, at this hour, but how worthwhile it had been!

Recognizing that God knew her on a first-name basis, she seldom used "canned" or simplistic prayers, but right now it seemed quite natural to just repeat what Jana said the evening before, when too moved to even begin enumerating her many blessings. "Thank You, God, for *everything.*"

And Rob, so loving and so aware of Vanessa's feelings, drew his wife close and whispered for her ears alone, "Amen!"

*   *   *   *   *

Dear Reader,

What a joy it is to be with you again as we revisit
Sylvan Falls, the friendly Pennsylvania town of
Gram McHenry and her family. We had met, in
A Family for Andi, the somewhat out-of-sync cousin,
Vanessa, who now holds an executive position in the
company formed by Andi and her genius father—and
it's *her* story we've just been sharing.

I've always been intrigued by the formative factors
making people who they are. Sometimes these are
obvious, and it's all too easy to say, often unjustly,
"Of *course,* what can one expect of somebody growing
up in that situation?"

But there are many hidden or unrealized situations,
events and secrets that can, as in Vanessa's life,
create barriers to establishing deep friendships—and
insecurities often threaten relationships with others, and
even with God.

I've been blessed to live for many years in a small
community where people are still genuinely concerned
for one another, and volunteerism is for many a way of
life. *Gram* would be at home here—and I suspect you
would be, too.

Thank you for spending this time in "my" world. I hope
it has been as pleasant an experience for you in reading
this as it's been for me as I wrote it.

Sincerely,

Eileen Berger

Next Month From Steeple Hill's

Love Inspired®

COURTING KATARINA
by
Carol Steward

THE *SEQUEL* TO
SECOND TIME AROUND

*Katarina Berthoff and Alex MacIntyre meet at the
wedding of her sister and his brother—and sparks
start to fly! But the beautiful dollmaker has a fear
of commitment, and the rugged forest firefighter
is ready to settle down and raise a family. Discover
how Alex convinces Kat that they're truly meant
to be together.*

**Don't miss
COURTING KATARINA
On sale April 2001**

Available at your favorite retail outlet.

Love Inspired®

Visit us at www.steeplehill.com   LICK

Next Month From Steeple Hill's

Love Inspired

THE MARRYING KIND
by

Cynthia Rutledge

*An important business merger is threatened by
an impossible ultimatum: Nick Lanagan must
date the boss's daughter or no deal! Nick
desperately enlists the lovely Taylor Rollins into
a pretend engagement to save the deal. Smart,
beautiful and faithful to the Lord, Taylor is
everything a man could want. Suddenly Nick
is struggling to keep their engagement
purely professional.*

**Don't miss
THE MARRYING KIND
On sale April 2001**

Available at your favorite retail outlet.

Love Inspired

Visit us at www.steeplehill.com   LITMK

Next Month
From Steeple Hill's

Love Inspired®

A HERO FOR KELSEY
by
Carolyne Aarsen

*After her husband died and left her and her
young son with nothing, Kelsey Swain found
herself working at her parents' diner. When her
husband's best friend, Will Dempsey, steps in to
lend a hand, an undeniable attraction between
them grows. But can Will convince her that
heroes really do exist?*

**Don't miss
A HERO FOR KELSEY
On sale April 2001**

Available at your favorite retail outlet.

Love Inspired®

Visit us at www.steeplehill.com   LIAHFK

Next Month
From Steeple Hill's

Love Inspired®

A BRIDE FOR DRY CREEK
by

Janet Tronstad

Book Three in the Dry Creek series

Once upon a time...there lived a young man and
a young woman who loved each other very much.
They married, but were pulled apart by evil forces.
However, they never stopped loving each other, even
after twenty years. When the woman found herself
in danger, the man suddenly returned to town to
rescue her. Can the people of Dry Creek help
this couple live happily ever after?

**Don't miss
A BRIDE FOR DRY CREEK
On sale May 2001**

 *Love Inspired®*

Visit us at www.steeplehill.com

LIBDC

Next month
From Steeple Hill's

Love Inspired®

FINALLY HOME
by
Lyn Cote

*In search of spiritual healing
after a broken engagement,
Hannah Kirkland decides to help her
parents move to their new home in
Wisconsin. But they arrive to find
their house half-finished—and a
handsome builder full of excuses!
Can Hannah and Guthrie stop
bickering long enough to
realize they may be
the perfect couple?*

**Don't miss
FINALLY HOME
On sale May 2001**

 *Love Inspired*®

Visit us at www.steeplehill.com
LIFH